Rattlesnake Rock

T. M. DOLAN

A Black Horse Western

ROBERT HALE · LONDON

ISBN 0 7090 7602 9

Robert Hale Limited
Clerkenwell House
Clerkenwell Green
London EC1R 0HT

Typeset by
Derek Doyle & Associates, Liverpool.
Printed and bound in Great Britain by
Antony Rowe Limited, Wiltshire

Rattlesnake Rock

The peaceful town of Rattlesnake Rock suffers a vicious chain reaction when hired killer Roscoe Lynx books into the local hotel. His reputation for seeking out his victim and killing him in self-defence keeps him within the law. Speculation as to whom he has come to kill soon leads to violence and a suicide.

A likeable man, Lynx makes friends with several people, including the sheriff, and becomes romantically involved with Melanie, the beautiful daughter of Judge Larne. But emotions are in turmoil, loyalties are brought into question, and the strain on the townsfolk becomes unbearable as Lynx finds a target and moves in for the kill.

ONE

Speculation was rife in the Blue Star saloon. It was a threat to the concentration of the four players in the game of poker. The saloon was crowded, ablaze with light and heavy with smoke. It was an establishment that afforded every facility for fools, young and old, to part with their money. The roughly hewn bar was the haunt of seasoned trail-herders and groups of empty-headed, grinning young cowboys just starting out on their careers of rowdiness and dissipation.

The remainder of the long room was dotted with round tables at which sat respectable local menfolk, drinking while they earnestly discussed business. Sitting at a corner table, the quartet of poker players somehow managed to isolate themselves mentally from the drunkenness, loud conversation, and disorderly conduct going on around them. Not far from them an argument over a girl developed into a fight. There was uproar in which a table was overturned. Glasses were smashed and the short, squealing screams of saloon girls added to the noise.

In air bluish with cigarette smoke, the four veteran gamblers were unmoved by the mayhem. The sharp-faced dealer looked questioningly at Major DeWitt, who answered the unspoken question silently with a shake of his white-haired head. He didn't want another card. Watching DeWitt over the top of his hand of cards, Lon Mackeever chuckled softly and drawled, ''You scared of being dealt the death card, Major?'

With an angry glare at Rattlesnake Rock's oddly remote, cynical, young lawyer, DeWitt retorted, 'This ain't no time for jokes, Mackeever. If it's true that Roscoe Lynx has ridden into town, then death has ridden in with him.'

'There sure isn't any *if* about it,' the third player, Denis Peers, the town's frailly built and perpetually nervous banker, spoke shakily in his cultured tones. 'He rode by Peter Henry's store as close as I'm sitting to you right now. He went into the Trails End, which must mean that he booked a room. I don't like it. Lynx is definitely in town, and it seems that he is here to stay. At least for some time.'

'And Lynx being about the most infamous hired gun this side of the Green River, means that there's a bullet in the chamber of his gun with the name of some poor cuss here in town on it,' DeWitt warned. With a frown he added, 'Beats me who it could be. I can't think of anybody in Rattlesnake Rock who someone would want dead.'

'Then you sure aren't thinking very hard, Major.'

Mackeever lazily raised his glass of whiskey, his eyes flicking over its rim at the major. With his black hair having a hint of a wave, and his brown, deep-set eyes, the good-looking young lawyer had supreme self-confidence. He used a jerk of his thumb to indicate the ornately dressed saloon proprietor Jake Herbert, who was behind his busy bar keeping his army of sweating barkeeps in order. 'There's Jake, for instance, who cheated poor old Isaac Penfold out of this place. Maybe Isaac got himself enough money together to hire Lynx to get his revenge for him. Then there's you, Denis, and that bank of yours. How many lives have you blighted by foreclosing on property around here?'

'That's all a very proper part of the business of banking,' Peers protested feebly. 'My bank operates in a scrupulously fair way.'

'Maybe so, but you've still made enemies, Denis,' Mackeever said, before pointing at Clive Wrexham, the suave card dealer, and going on, 'You, Clive, you don't always deal from the top of the deck. There's quite a few who have gone out of here swearing to get even with you. That brings me to you, Major. You don't show up as a good neighbour, having forced Jim Carter to sell his land to you. That deal made your Six-Bar ranch twice the size at a tenth of the price.'

Head bowed, Major DeWitt jiggled the glass he held in small circles, studying the moving liquor like it was the most interesting thing in the world. Then he challenged the lawyer. 'And what of you, Mackeever, you smug shyster? The fact that you're going to marry Judge Larne's daughter doesn't put you above us. We know nothing about you before you came to Rattlesnake Rock: could be that your past is catching up with you.'

'That's very true, Major,' Mackeever agreed, with an affable nod. 'Each and everyone of us has a past, which means that any one of us could be the man Roscoe Lynx is after. But you are so accustomed to seeing me carrying books and papers that you haven't noticed that I always pack a six-gun.'

'Are you saying you'd be a match for Lynx if it's you he's come for?' Clive Wrexham sneered.

'If it should be me, then I guess we'll find that out all in good time,' Mackeever answered coolly, his expensive clothing unable to hide the fact that he had a muscle-packed physique to complement his good looks.

'Whoever it is,' the banker observed gloomily, 'he'll be dead when Lynx rides out of town.'

With an angry snort, the major declared, 'No, he won't, because we're not going to let it happen. Max Angier, my foreman, could take care of this Lynx *hombre* on his own, but I'll take no chances. I'll send some of the boys in with Max and have them run Lynx out of town.'

Mackeever gave a discouraging shake of his head. 'That's not a good idea, Major. Your foreman isn't in Roscoe Lynx's class. You'd finished up with Angier and your other hands lying dead on the street.'

'Then we'll get Sheriff Winters to handle this,' the rancher compromised.

'Which will mean Lynx will kill Mike Winters before gunning down the man he's after and riding out of town,' an amused Mackeever commented.

'Sheriff Winters is a good man.'

'He'll be a dead man if he goes up against Roscoe Lynx, Major,' Mackeever predicted laconically.

'You seem to know a lot about this Lynx, Mackeever,' Denis Peers said, his thin white hands shaking as they held his cards.

With a shrug, Mackeever replied, 'I just know his reputation, the same as you men. But that's enough for me.'

'So, what are you going to do,' DeWitt asked contemptuously, 'crawl away in a hole and hide until Lynx leaves town.'

'That sounds like the best idea,' Mackeever said, and the other three couldn't be certain whether or not he was joking. Then he asked, 'Are we playing poker or aren't we?'

Throwing his card face down on the table, Major DeWitt said, 'We're not. Sheriff Winters has just come in the door. Let's hear what he has to say about this Lynx business.'

Standing up from the table, the major beckoned to Mike Winters, who was a quiet, reserved man for all his record as a fighter. His appearance made it difficult to believe that he could use his fists or a gun with deadly effect. The sheriff had a lithe and gracefully formed physique and features of aquiline regularity.

Acknowledging DeWitt's signal, with a curt nod, he headed for the group of card players, moving in the sure way of a man who has absolute control over every sinew and muscle of his body.

The Trail's End was a credit to an obviously thriving town. It was situated in a secluded spot buried deep among trees just off Rattlesnake Rock's wide main street. Its renown for good food made it the favourite eating-house of local people. The low-ceilinged place had atmosphere, plenty of it. It was well patronized now at early evening. Dining regularly at the Trail's End was something of a social statement in the town.

Judge Larne and his daughters Melanie and Elizabeth sat at their usual table, which was always reserved for them. They exchanged friendly smiles with the plain-looking and painfully shy Miss Carter, the town's schoolteacher, who, as always, sat alone.

The talk going on around them was confined to one subject. News of the arrival of a hired gun in town had travelled fast. The conversations were a blend of excitement and fear.

Quickly scanning the room, Melanie, the elder of the judge's daughters whispered, 'He's not here.'

A lack of symmetry in Melanie's features defied a description of beautiful, but she was stunningly attractive. Dark-complexioned, her black hair, worn long, was pulled back and tied with a single red ribbon. The folk of Rattlesnake Rock couldn't understand why Melanie was still unattached, while the less striking and younger Elizabeth was betrothed to Lon Mackeever, the prosperous lawyer.

'How would you know, Melanie?' Elizabeth questioned her sister. 'You haven't any idea what he looks like.'

'Rough and tough, I would imagine. Isn't that right, Dad?' Melanie said.

Dabbing at his nose with a folded white handkerchief that was quickly stained by blood that was startlingly crimson, the judge looked at her dubiously. 'I've seen them come in all shapes and sizes, Melanie. This is a badly frightened town. Men like Lynx are an abomination, and I pray that we are able to have our dinner without having sight of him.'

'It looks as if Rita Duprez is hoping he'll be along,' Elizabeth said, with a small and secret grin.

She had indicated a woman sitting at a table beside a window. With a heavily painted face, she had blonde hair piled high on her head. The shapely, cool and aloof Rita Duprez owned a small theatre at the far end of town, an establishment graced by highly cultured, musically gifted young ladies. Named the Golden Arts, the theatre, it was claimed but never proved, was a front for a lucrative bordello. Most of the townsfolk regarded Rita as one of the Crimson Sisterhood.

'She's most probably aiming to make Max Angier jealous,' Melanie suggested. She glanced at a grandfather clock. 'He usually comes in around this time when he's in town.'

'I don't care to hear my daughters discussing the likes of Rita Duprez,' Judge Larne complained, still using his now badly stained handkerchief to staunch the flow of blood from his nose.

'Are you all right, Dad?' Elizabeth worriedly asked.

'It's worse than usual, isn't it?'

Judge Larne suffered from nosebleeds whenever he was under pressure. Dr Baron, the town's physician, had explained that the bleeding was a good thing, a safety valve. A stroke was the alternative, the doctor said. Though her father was respected as a fair man, Elizabeth wondered if he was unduly stressed by the arrival of the man they called Roscoe Lynx. Judges were known to be targets for those seeking revenge.

The judge smiled at her reassuringly, although he suddenly looked very old, very tired. 'I've had work this afternoon that has been particularly taxing. That's what brought this on. It's not serious but just inconvenient at this time. I'm sure it will have stopped by the time dinner is served.'

'I hope so, for ...' Melanie began, but didn't finish what she was going to say.

A hush had descended on the gathering as a man walked down the hotel stairs and entered the dining-room. Everyone there knew that this had to be Roscoe Lynx, the man whose name had been whispered fearfully around Rattlesnake Rock all afternoon. But the stranger wasn't what anyone had expected.

Resplendent in an olive-green jacket and darker green cravat complementing a high-collared shirt, he wore his fair hair long and was incredibly handsome. Of no more than average height, he walked to a window table with impeccable poise. Pulling out a chair, he sat facing the door. To the amazement of everyone there, he appeared to be unarmed.

Nothing about the gentlemanly newcomer fitted the menacing images they had created of Roscoe Lynx. The reality left them uncertain whether to feel cheated or relieved.

The silence in the dining-room remained after the man who had caused it was seated. All were keenly aware that the unnatural quiet was very noticeable and extremely impolite. But the effect of Lynx's appearance had been so profound that everyone present found it was impossible to resume normal conversation. Only the soft footfalls of the hotel's two harassed waitresses disturbed the embarrassing silence.

Apparently oblivious to the effect his entrance had, Lynx slowly unfolded a napkin and sat calmly waiting for his order to be taken.

'You know him?'

'I know *of* him, Major,' Sheriff Winters corrected DeWitt.

'Whatever, Sheriff,' the major brushed aside what he regarded as a minor technicality. 'What we all know is that this is a town of peaceable, peace-loving folk who don't deserve to have a murderer in their midst.

'Lynx is not a murderer, Major.'

'I can't believe that you are taking his side, Sheriff.'

'I don't take sides, Major.' Winters spoke quietly and evenly. 'I am merely stating that Roscoe Lynx has committed no crime here in Rattlesnake Rock or anywhere else.'

'You'll be telling me next that he's not a hired gun,' the major snorted angrily.

'You are a stubborn, argumentative cuss, Major,' Lon Mackeever said mildly. 'Mike won't be telling you that, because Lynx *is* a hired gun. But he has never murdered anyone.'

The sheriff nodded. 'That's true. All those Lynx ever shot made the first move.'

'So he's not a wanted man,' Denis Peers said worriedly. 'That means you can do nothing about him being here, Sheriff Winters?'

'I can't throw a man in the hoosegow just because folk don't like having him around.'

'Be that as it may,' Major DeWitt argued. The lines of discontent and bitterness on his face became deeper and more distorting. 'The only solution in all situations such as this is to fight fire with fire, and that's what I intend to do.'

'I don't want any of this kind of talk, gentlemen,' Sheriff Winters cautioned. 'You employ a lot of men on the Six-Bar, Major, and some of them are mighty tough *hombres*. Don't make the mistake of having them break the law where Lynx is concerned. The same goes for you, Wrexham. Don't be tempted to use that .38 you carry in that shoulder holster. You, Mackeever, are perfectly capable of taking care of yourself, but don't try it in my town whatever the provocation.'

'Seems to me that you're handing out the wrong advice, Sheriff,' DeWitt protested. 'What do you expect us to do?'

'I want everyone in town to stay calm and make no

attempt to defend themselves if approached by Lynx.'

Denis Peers ordinarily pale face seemed even whiter as he enquired, 'You're saying that the man he's after should sacrifice himself for the good of the town?'

'I'm saying nothing of the sort,' Winters responded heatedly. 'The fact is that Roscoe Lynx will deliberately provoke his intended victim so as to be able to claim self-defence. He won't go for his gun until he goads the other man into making a move, an absolutely foolish move.'

'His last move,' Mackeever added for effect.

'Exactly,' the sheriff acknowledged.

'What if he's come to Rattlesnake Rock for you, Sheriff Winters, will you be doing what you want us to do?' the major asked.

Using a forefinger to tap the silver star pinned to his chest, the sheriff replied, 'This makes it different for me, Major.'

'I don't need no badge, Sheriff. I'm ready to face Lynx alone,' DeWitt blustered, as much a propagandist as the next man, and propaganda meant convincing someone else of the truth of something you knew to be a lie.

With a dismissive shrug, Mike Winters turned and walked away. Watching him go, the major commented, 'I do believe our sheriff lacks the craw for a showdown with Roscoe Lynx.'

'You're much older than me, Major,' Lon Mackeever remarked, 'but you sure haven't learned much about men in your time.'

'Are you saying that I'm wrong about Sheriff Winters, Mackeever?'

'I'd say you were half right, Major. But don't sell Winters short. It's probably true that he doesn't want a showdown with Lynx, he'd be loco if he did, but he won't dodge it if it should come to that.'

'I happen to think that you're wrong, Mackeever,' Major DeWitt said. 'Very wrong.'

'That's your prerogative, Major,' Mackeever smiled. 'Could be that everyone here in Rattlesnake Rock is wrong about Roscoe Lynx. The problem is that one of us is never going to know whether he was right or wrong.'

'That unfortunate person could be you, Mackeever,' the major took pleasure in pointing out.

'As a gambling man I'm ready to lay odds on it being you first choice, Major, with Denis the money-man a close second,' the still smiling lawyer countered. 'Whichever one of you it is, I'll make certain that you have a nice funeral.'

'I don't think having this killer in town is something to joke about,' Peers protested anxiously.

'Who's joking?' Mackeever chuckled.

Having lost all interest in the poker game, all four men then sat quietly, lost in their own thoughts.

Accustomed to the reaction his arrival in town always provoked, Roscoe Lynx had paid no attention to the awkward atmosphere his presence had created in the dining-room. Feeling the tension in a town build steadily was a common experience. The diners

16

around him and the townsfolk away from the hotel were frantically wondering which of them had brought him to Rattlesnake Rock. They were in for a long wait to find out. Before he could do the job he had come to Rattlesnake Rock to do, he first had to find evidence that would identify the man he had been sent to kill.

Ever watchful, he had seen the sheriff come in to sit at a corner table that enabled him to see not only the whole room, but the entrance as well. That told Lynx much about the local lawman he had already marked down as a natural fighting man. The sheriff's deft, sure movements were innate, not learned. That made him dangerous.

His meal over, Lynx was finishing his coffee when a blonde with tall hair who had been sitting at a nearby table approached. Uninvited, she sat down across the table from him.

'As I'm sure that we'll meet at some time, and as I am not one to stand on ceremony,' the blonde said, 'I'll introduce myself. I'm Rita Duprez.'

Not answering, Lynx drained his coffee cup. Rattlesnake Rock was the same as every other place. Fear had those with reason to feel most guilty, but who were incapable of enduring the waiting without knowing, want to push him into revealing if they were his reason for being in town. He had no interest in Rita Duprez, professional or otherwise.

Looking past him out of the window, she said, 'I love the view from here at this time of day. Those distant mountains first turn purple, and then they become outlined in gold.'

'Can you see the view from the table where you were sitting?' he asked.

'Yes.' Despite its hardness, her painted face flushed a little.

Abruptly standing up she stood glaring at him for a moment, then she walked haughtily away and out of the room. Aware that he had made an enemy, Lynx was content. You knew exactly where you stood with those who hated you. Fathoming the friendly ones was difficult, if not impossible.

Sensing someone looking at him intently, an alert Lynx placed who it was without looking either to his left or right. A black-haired young woman sitting at a table with a girl and an elderly man was studying him. Turning his head quickly he locked eyes with her for a fleeting moment. She turned her face away swiftly, but not before he had read something with which he was familiar in her dark eyes. It told him that his stay in this town could well be an enjoyable one.

A young waitress, afraid of him by the talk she had heard, hovered nervously by his table. She enquired with trepidation, 'More coffee, sir?'

As she refilled his cup he put a dollar bill on the table close to her, and asked conversationally, 'Who is the elderly gentleman sitting with the two young ladies?'

'That's Judge Larne and his daughters, Melanie and Elizabeth.'

'Is Melanie the one with the red ribbon in her hair.'

Eyes twinkling, the waitress smiled cheekily at

Lynx. She was relaxed in his company now that his interest in Melanie Larne proved that he was human and not the monster she had been led to believe.

'That's Melanie,' she confirmed.

TWO

As the tough ramrod of the Six-Bar ranch and a man who belonged in the great outdoors, Max Angier always felt gauche and ill-mannered when visiting Rita Duprez. He had never become accustomed to being ushered into her tastefully furnished parlour, where a uniformed black maid politely took his coat and hat. Rita's attitude towards him made it worse. Though she always poured him champagne, she did it as if she was putting a dish of water down for a dog. Yet Angier was so besotted with her that he meekly took her insults and off-hand manner. He would put up with anything just to be with her.

This evening she was in a foul mood. A stranger to the town had wounded her outsized self-love. Angier had already heard plenty about this stranger from his boss, Major DeWitt. DeWitt was completely obsessed with Roscoe Lynx, but the rancher's hatred paled into insignificance when compared to Rita's barely suppressed furious loathing.

'Lynx is a hired killer, Rita,' Angier warned. 'Best if you keep away from him.'

''He's a dandy,' she sneered. 'An overdressed fop.'

'Maybe, but he's still a hired gun,' Angier advised, coming as close as he dared to arguing with her.

'I've seen him, and he's nothing,' she said sulkily. 'I don't know why every goddamn man in the town, including you, Max, is so afraid of him.'

Hurt by her criticism, Angier was about to retort that he wasn't afraid of Lynx or any other man. But he stopped himself, suspecting that there was more than being snubbed that had her in such a state about Lynx. Rita Duprez was a dangerous person who used people to gain her own ends. It was likely that she suspected that she was Lynx's reason for being in town, and was trying to goad him into gunplay with the hired killer.

'You see! You don't deny it, Max,' she shouted. 'You're as terrified as the rest of them. What sort of man are you? A gutless braggart too timid to stand up for your woman?'

'But you are not my woman,' Angier protested. 'I've always wanted you to be, but you've always pushed me away.'

'That's because I am a real woman, Max Angier, which means that I need a real man,' she said. 'I know how to show respect once a man has proved himself to me.'

'What are you saying, Rita?'

Even though he was a hard man, totally fearless, Angier was uneasy by the direction in which Rita was steering the conversation. He had never, and would never, back away from a fight. But though he adored Rita Duprez, he would not allow her or any other

21

woman to push him into a life-or-death situation.

'Let me pour you another drink, Max,' she purred, as soft as a kitten, 'and I'll tell you exactly what I'm saying.'

Calmer now, she looked absolutely beautiful in the golden lamplight. Angier obediently held out his empty glass, but Rita gave a little shake of her head. 'I'm sorry for the things I said this evening, Max, but it has cleared the air between us. Come, bring your glass and we'll go somewhere much more comfortable to drink together.'

Her big eyes were on him, questioning, teasing and possibly even mocking. Angier didn't hesitate to follow her up a flight of majestic stairs. Intrigued by the mystery of it all, certain now that he was heading for a romantic tryst, he had completely forgotten the way she had been manipulating him just a few minutes earlier.

But he wasn't prepared for the disorienting effect the room that he entered had on him. He was completely out of his top-cowhand depth. It was a scented boudoir with a bed that was fantastically large to his idea of such things. Heavy drapes of crimson velvet covered the window. The opulent surroundings weakened his self-confidence, creating an unusual diffidence. He instantly and unhappily became the unsophisticated cowboy that he really was.

Jake Herbert had risen from bar swamp to gambler. Even though he could neither read nor write, he had made a fortune out of Herbert House, the gambling saloon he had opened in El Paso. A dark, lean, cigar smoker, he was a man with a creative mind. This was evident in the way he had built the Blue Star on moving to Rattlesnake Rock. He did things in style and his saloon was a grand place. There was a lavishly furnished room at the rear that could be reached from a hallway made by a screen. This meant that a gentleman could take a female acquaintance for a drink without either of them being seen by the riffraff drinking at the bar.

Herbert had wealth, property, and respect. Too intelligent to ever become belligerent, he kept his saloon virtually trouble free. But he did have two glaring faults: one was his possessive attitude towards Gabriella Fernandez, who was the saloon's enter-tainer and his live-in partner, and the other was a talent for over-dramatizing.

He spoke worriedly now to Lon Mackeever, who was leaning nonchalantly on the bar.

'Every time I think back to when I started out in El Paso, Mackeever, I'm sure that I'm the one Lynx has come for,' Herbert said.

'That's what just about every other man in town is sure of, Jake,' Mackeever smiled.

'Including you, Lon?'

'I've considered it a possibility,' Mackeever admit-ted.

'Doesn't he worry you?'

'They say he was dressed like a real gentleman at dinner in the Trails End this evening.'

'That don't make no difference,' Herbert argued. 'I hear this Roscoe Lynx is one *mal hombre*.'

'So was Billy the Kid, but I called him out one night down in Sante Fe and he didn't show.'

'Billy the Kid was afraid of you?' Jake Herbert was in awe.

Shrugging, Mackeever modestly replied, 'Who knows? Maybe he just wasn't feeling good right then.'

A roar of applause filled the saloon then as Gabriella Fernandez came out on the small stage. A sultry dark-skinned, smouldering-eyed *señorita*, she held just about every man there under her spell. All she appeared to be wearing, which barely covered a superb figure, was a short red jacket and black stockings supported by fancy garters. Gabriella had a good voice, too. There was silence as she began to sing the all-time favourite 'Home Sweet Home'.

Savouring the haunting song, pleasantly lost for a moment, Mackeever suddenly became aware that Jake Herbert was signalling frantically but secretly to him. He looked to see that a stranger who had to be Roscoe Lynx had entered the saloon. Casually dressed now in a plain blue shirt and dark trousers, Lynx pushed his Stetson back a little on his head and walked to the bar. As he approached, Mackeever noted the six-gun that was worn low on his lean hips and tied down. He stopped close to Mackeever.

'Can I buy you a drink, mister?' Mackeever asked. 'Sort of welcome you to town.'

'I don't usually get a welcome.'

'I don't usually buy strangers a drink.'

'Then why break your own rules for me?' Lynx enquired, friendly like.

Mackeever grinned. 'I guess I kinda figured that if

I am the one you've been hired to gun down, then you wouldn't shoot a man who stood you a drink.'

'If you think that, you are wasting your money,' Lynx said, with a soft, brief laugh. 'But I will drink with you if you'll do me a favour.'

'What's that?'

'I've got a real fancy for a couple of hands of poker,' Lynx answered. He looked across to where Clive Wrexham sat dealing cards, the squirrel tail of his profession in his hat. 'Not with the houseman. Just you and me, a quiet game.'

'Suits me; I'm Lon Mackeever.'

'Roscoe Lynx,' the gunfighter introduced himself.

It was only when Mackeever saw Jake Herbert hurrying away from the bar that he realized that Gabriella had stopped singing in mid-song and the music had trailed away soon afterwards. Now just the three musicians who had accompanied her were standing bewildered on the stage. Gabriella had disappeared.

Going up the stairs of the saloon's private quarters two at a time, Jake Herbert could hear Gabriella weeping before he opened the door. With a bag half packed beside her, she sat on the bed holding her head in her hands.

'What happened, Gabriella?' he cried. 'Why did you rush off like that?'

Sitting beside her, he slipped an arm around her shoulders, feeling them heave as she wept. Trying to speak, she choked on her words, cleared her throat, then burst into tears again. Herbert waited patiently.

Several minutes went by before she was able to speak.

'That man who came into the saloon when I was singing, Jake.'

'Roscoe Lynx?'

'Yes,' she said, surprised. 'Do you know him?'

Perturbed, Herbert shook his head. 'No. I'd neither seen nor heard of him before today. It's plain that you know him, Gabriella.'

'Yes, another time another place, long before I met you,' she confessed.

Misunderstanding, reasoning that she was upset that he would learn that she had once been involved with a gunfighter, Herbert spoke consolingly. 'Your life before we knew each other is your business, Gabriella.'

'It's not that, Jake, it's not that,' she sobbed. 'I am the reason he has come to Rattlesnake Rock.'

'I think I understand. You left him, and now you believe that he's come to get you.'

Come to get Gabriella? His chances of being Lynx's victim had just doubled. Herbert felt panic rise up in him. Though Roscoe Lynx was handsome and friendly in manner, the very sight of him had struck fear into Herbert's heart. His mouth went dry now and a tic started up on the right side of his face. But his terror eased down as he heard what Gabriella was saying.

'No. No. No!' she replied agitatedly. 'I didn't leave him. He used me as a stake in a two-horse race, and lost. I ran away from Nathan Leaming, the man who won me. He was a rich merchant, and a very jealous man. It is Leaming who must be paying Lynx to come

26

here and kill me. I must get away.'

'No, Gabriella. That would solve nothing, as he would follow you.'

'Then what can I do?' Gabriella wailed.

Holding her tight, Herbert said, 'I need time to think. But you stay here where I can take care of you. We need to find out for sure that it is you that Lynx is after.'

'It could be too late then,' she sobbed.

'It won't be. We'll work something out, Gabriella. Don't you worry.'

Rita Duprez's house stood on the extreme lower edge of town. Facing a long walk through a fast descending dusk, Max Angier didn't hurry as he negotiated a poorly lit, narrow, squalid and mean street before passing through the shadowy Donovan's Lane between the Golden Arts theatre and the feed store to reach the wide, dusty main street. Though his pace was slow his determination was diamond hard. It went beyond his promise to Rita. It was a matter of pride, and he was a very proud man. He had long been aware that the way he trailed along behind Rita Duprez made him thought of as being as weak as a hind-tit calf. He was about to show them how wrong they were. A man is often judged by the desirability of his woman and having the famously lovely Rita Duprez on his arm tomorrow would enhance Max Angier's reputation.

Walking on, he passed by the grey-and-white-robed nuns intoning their prayers in the grounds of the sombre Mission of the Sisters of Mercy. The holy sisters parading on a beautifully kept lawn were oblivious to the harsh lives of men such as Angier and the wickedness of the pleasure-seekers of the town who ignored the donations box affixed to the mission gate when they passed by.

Max Angier noticed neither the holy sisters nor the donations box as he strolled resolutely on towards the brightly lit doorways of the Blue Star saloon.

It was possible to learn more about a man by observing him than it was by listening to what he had to say. Roscoe Lynx had begun learning about Lon Mackeever from the moment they had moved to a small table and he had taken the chair in which he could sit with his back to the wall. Mackeever had told him that he was a lawyer. But no lawyer would have been so disturbed by having to sit with his back exposed. As a tense Mackeever broke open the new deck of cards he had obtained from a barkeep, Lynx said quietly, 'Relax, Mackeever. I'll watch your back for you.'

They cut for dealer, and Mackeever had the highest card. He spoke as he dealt the cards. 'Why should I worry about my back?'

'For the same reason,' Lynx suggested, 'that you wear that gunbelt and .45 under that long coat of yours. You've been more than a lawyer in your time, Mackeever.'

As he fanned the cards he held, Lynx surreptitiously watched Mackeever for a reaction. He was rewarded not by any show of fear, but the instant alertness learned in the school of the survival of the fittest and the fastest.

Having placed his glass of whiskey on the table at his left hand when he had taken his seat, Lynx now knocked his hand against it as if by accident. As the glass was about to spill its contents, Mackeever, in a chain-lighting series of movements, laid down his cards and his right hand flashed out to steady the toppling glass before retrieving his cards.

Though Lynx's face was expressionless, Mackeever sensed he had been tested. He asked lazily, 'Is it me, Lynx? Am I the man that had you ride into Rattlesnake Rock?'

Shaking his head reprovingly, Lynx replied, 'As a lawyer, Mackeever, you should know all about privileged information.'

'If it is me, if I'm your mark, then you'll need to be fast, Lynx, real fast.'

'I already figured that,' Lynx shrugged. 'But maybe it isn't you. Could be that narrow-faced coot dealing for the house over there.'

'Clive Wrexham,' Mackeever identified the card dealer. He added a suggestion of his own. 'Maybe it's Jake Herbert who owns this joint.'

'Perhaps. Or that white-faced, sick-looking critter sitting in on the card game.'

'That's Denis Peers, who runs the bank,' Mackeever said, aware that Peers was eyeing them anxiously. 'You sure got a funny way of asking a whole heap of questions, Lynx.'

'It goes with the job.' Lynx permitted himself a slight twitching of the lips that could have developed into a smile but didn't. 'You aren't obliged to give me answers.'

'If I were, then you wouldn't be getting any.'

With a soft chuckle, Lynx said, 'I kind of figured that for myself. Just one last question, Mackeever, then we'll settle down and have ourselves some real card-playing. Is the Six-Bar rancher in here?'

'Major DeWitt? No, the major's not here tonight, Lynx. Did Jim Cutler hire you?'

Lynx avoided giving an answer by asking a question of his own. 'Is Cutler a friend of yours, Mackeever?'

'I knew him and respected him when he lived hereabouts,' Mackeever replied. 'Is DeWitt the one you're after?'

'Would you believe me if I told you that right now I don't rightly know who it is?'

'I believe you,' Mackeever answered, 'but I don't want to, as it means that I could still be the one.'

'I'd really hate it if that proved to be true,' Lynx said, dully. 'Come on, let's get down to some serious poker.'

They had been playing for around twenty minutes, and Mackeever was winning, when Lynx lightly touched his foot against Mackeever's under the table. Barely moving his lips, he said, 'Don't turn around. A *hombre*'s just come in who looks like trouble for either you or me.'

'What's he look like?' Mackeever enquired, softly.

'A big guy, broad-shouldered, deep-chested, dressed in a charcoal-grey suit, white shirt and a dark string tie.'

30

'That's Max Angier, the major's ramrod, Lynx. I guess DeWitt's sent him into town to brace you,' Mackeever said. 'It's about to start, Lynx, and it will continue until you leave town.' He added a warning. 'I make my living in Rattlesnake Rock, so I can't get involved.'

'I don't recall asking you for help,' Lynx said, flatly. A sudden hush had fallen on the assembly. 'I don't need to tell you to move slowly, Mackeever, so just get up and stand aside.'

There was now no music, no drone of mass conversation. The only sound was the skidding slide of a glass sent speeding down the counter to a customer by a nervous barkeep. Young and athletic, Angier made his way towards Lynx. He walked with quick, short steps, the weight of his body shifting rhythmically to either heel. With a slight swagger to it that was a challenge in itself, it was the walk of a fighting man.

Unwilling to look away, none of them wanting to miss a moment of the drama being played out before them, the saloon crowd parted by walking backwards. A safety area was cleared, as Max Angier came to a halt facing a still seated Lynx. Angier had a wild light in his eye. He was the kind of man who wore cuts and bruises like they were medals awarded in a war.

'Are you Roscoe Lynx?'

Quickly scanning the gathering, Lynx wondered if it included any Six-Bar men there willing to back Angier. He had long ago learned how swiftly a crisis can make what looks like a nameless and featureless crowd break up into a number of distinctive and easily recognizable individuals with individual loyalties.

'That's me,' Lynx coolly replied. Holding both hands high in a non-threatening gesture, he rose slowly to his feet. 'You here to do DeWitt's fighting for him?'

'This has nothing to do with the major, Lynx. This is strictly between you and me.'

Frowning, giving a little shake of his head, Lynx said, 'You got me beat there, *amigo*. I don't know you. Why should I want to kill a man I don't know?'

'You're pretty damned sure of yourself, stranger,' Angier said flatly.

Lynx's two words were just audible, 'Try me.'

Angier's hand went down above the handle of his holstered six-shooter, fingers crooked like claws. He was held in that pose by the sound of the saloon doors being pushed open. Sheriff Winters stepped in to take up a neutral stance.

The sheriff's arrival registered as a fleeting distraction in Max Angier's eyes. Taking advantage of this, Lynx used both of his hands to vault over the table with the agility of a mountain lion. Angier had drawn his gun, and he triggered off a shot as Lynx came sailing through the air at him. The bullet passed close to Lynx to bury itself in the wall.

Lynx collided with such force against Angier that the Six-Bar foreman was forced to take running steps backwards until his back crashed against the bar. Though Lynx landed sure-footed, it took him a split second to find his balance. Seeing what he believed to be an opening, Angier rushed in. But Lynx was fast, extremely fast. As the Six-Bar man surged forwards on the attack, Lynx ducked low and grabbed him by the ankles. With bewildering speed, Lynx threw his opponent clean over his head.

Angier landed face down, slamming against the hard ground, the breath momentarily knocked out of him. But he instinctively rolled over quickly on to his back. Walking over, Lynx put a foot on the big man's throat and said, 'It's a mistake to shoot at me, Angier, and an even bigger mistake to miss.' Then he stepped back lazily, propping himself on the bar with both elbows as he waited for Angier to get up.

The local man climbed to his feet, and the crowd roared encouragement as he waded in with both fists, left and right, left and right. But his punches disturbed nothing but the air. The fast-moving Lynx was an elusive target. He also swiftly proved what a brilliant counter-puncher he was. A rock-hard fist slammed into Angier's face, laying the cheek open to the bone.

Stunned, Angier first sank to his knees and then collapsed on to his back. Reaching up with his right arm, his fingers trying to get a grip on the bar, Angier was in trouble. The gaping opening in his face leaked blood fast. Grabbing his opponent's upraised arm by the wrist with both hands, Lynx put a booted foot in Angier's armpit, then yanked hard on the arm. Hard men among the watching crowd winced at Angier's agonized groan as his shoulder was pulled out of joint.

There was a silence so deep that it was oppressive. No one there could credit the speed at which Lynx had demolished the powerfully built Angier. When Lynx had walked a few steps away, several men stooped to help the crippled man up from the floor. Mackeever stood waiting with Lynx's drink in his hand. He handed it to him.

Taking it, Lynx calmly remarked, 'It will be a while before he goes for his gun again.'

'Why didn't you kill him?' Mackeever asked.

'Because nobody was paying me to do so,' Lynx replied coldly.

THREE

'For a man just days away from marrying into the local aristocracy, so to speak, Lon, you are careless about the company you keep,' Sheriff Winters remarked. 'Roscoe Lynx isn't exactly popular with the good folk of Rattlesnake Rock.'

Leaning on the hitching rail outside his office, the sheriff and Mackeever watched the town go about its business at the start of a new day. There was a different atmosphere in Rattlesnake Rock that morning. The town had been shocked into staring silence. Everyone had been affected in some way by the trouble in the Blue Star the previous night. Though accustomed to the relatively harmless rowdiness from cowboys on pay nights, the townsfolk were uneasy at violence on that scale. Those who were there had witnessed the agony of Max Angier when Doc Ed Baron had knelt on the saloon floor to put his shoulder joint back into its socket. Those who had not been there had since had that harrowing episode luridly described to them. Roscoe Lynx had changed the tempo of life in the town. No one knew what to make of it all.

The sheriff had known what to make of it immediately the first slanting rays of the sun had awakened him that morning. They had streaked across the rooftops and had been reflected from the glass windows of the stores that stood across the street from the building that was both his home and his office. He had known then that a new era had dawned for Rattlesnake Rock. The Lynx problem was destined to get worse before it was over. It was likely to get a whole heap worse, and it was his responsibility.

'It was Angier who was on the prod, Mike,' Mackeever reminded the sheriff. 'Lynx avoided a shoot-out.'

Winters nodded. 'I know that. Lynx broke no laws last night, and he won't do so while he's here in town. That's not his style, Lon. It's the others who worry me. The major will be all horns and rattles over his top hand taking a beating. I just hope he's got the sense to stay out of town.'

'He'll be here on Saturday, Mike. He's a guest at the wedding. Everybody who is somebody in the county will be there.'

'That shouldn't be a problem as he'll be alone then,' the sheriff said. 'Even a hot-tempered old cuss like DeWitt wouldn't be foolish enough to take on Roscoe Lynx man-to-man. My worry is that he'll bring a bunch of men to set about Lynx. If that happens, then I'll have to take Lynx's side against the Six-Bar boys.'

'Let's hope it won't come to that, Mike.'

'Maybe Lynx'll do whatever he's come to do and ride out before anything like that can happen,' Winters wished aloud. 'Did he mention to you who it is he's after, Lon?'

'What I could make of it is that he's got some finding out to do before he knows.' Mackeever replied. He pointed down the street. 'There he is now.'

The two of them watched Roscoe Lynx step out of the hotel, look casually about him, and then walk off slowly towards the south end of the street.

Though the courtroom was much less formal when not in session, Melanie Larne was, as always, a little overpowered by her environment. Her legs felt shaky as she walked along the dark corridor with her sister. She was the only one of her family to be sensitive to atmosphere, and she regarded it as a curse. It had to be that some terrible things had taken place in the building when Rattlesnake Rock had first been settled, before the town had become civilized. Though her father was a scrupulously fair judge who had uplifted the area's judiciary by the way he operated, Melanie had never been at ease with the work that he did.

Elizabeth now led the way confidently into their father's chambers that had a refined appearance totally unexpected in a Western town. The plain walls were painted a clean, pale blue. The highly polished, heavy table was huge and uncluttered. Seated at the table when they entered was Judge Larne and Denis Peers.

Melanie was ill at ease by the banker's presence. Despite being a shy, reserved man, Peers made it obvious how he felt about her. Melanie knew that it was the dearest wish of her parents that she would one day marry him. To become the wife of the local banker would be the greatest gift she could ever give her bedridden mother, and not doing so burdened Melanie with guilt. But Denis Peers didn't appeal to her in the slightest, and she couldn't bring herself to sacrifice the rest of her life, even for her beloved mother.

'I'm sorry, Daddy,' Elizabeth apologized. 'We didn't know that you had someone with you.'

'Don't worry,' her father smiled. 'What can I do for you girls?'

Peers raised himself part way up from his chair. 'It's all right, Judge Larne. I'll leave you with your family.'

'Indeed you won't,' Larne said, waving a hand to gesture the banker back into his seat. 'We have matters to discuss that are important to you, Denis. Whatever it is that Melanie and Elizabeth want of me won't take long.' He looked lovingly and question- ingly at Elizabeth.

'It's just that I won't feel right unless we invite Auntie Ruth on Saturday, Daddy.'

Chewing on his bottom lip, the judge said dubi- ously, 'As I said before, girls, my sister doesn't take kindly to travel. However, it's your big day, Elizabeth, so if that is what you want I'll get in touch with Ruth as soon as my business with Mr Peers is concluded. I'll probably be able to persuade her to take the stage, particularly if I say that she can stay with us for a while.'

'Thanks, Daddy.' Elizabeth smiled happily, lunging forwards with the intention of hugging her father, then stopping herself on remembering where she was. Face suddenly serious, she asked worriedly, 'You don't think that this man everyone is talking about will spoil things on Saturday?'

'Of course not, why should he?' the judge answered with a small laugh. 'Whatever business he had in town is no concern of ours. Anyway, your husband-to-be is more than capable of taking care of you. In addition to Lon, Mike Winters will be among your guests, so you couldn't be in safer hands.'

'I realize that. It's just that everyone in town seems to be so frightened this morning,' Elizabeth said.

Melanie recalled, with a thrill that she tried to deny but couldn't, having seen the enigmatic, handsome and exciting Roscoe Lynx while dining at the hotel. She couldn't understand what all the fuss was about. A man with Roscoe's looks, impeccable sense of dress, and gracious style could not be the dangerous killer it was claimed that he was.

Aware that the banker frequented the town's most popular saloon, curiosity had Melanie ask, 'Were you at the Blue Star last night when that incident occurred, Mr Peers?'

Pleased at having been noticed by her, Peers nodded. Nervousness kept his head going up and down until he stopped it by pretending to rest his chin on his hand. 'I was, I regret to say, Miss Larne. It was ugly. Most brutal.'

'We neither want nor expect that kind of thing in Rattlesnake Rock,' Judge Larne said regretfully. 'Nevertheless, we must not permit it to grow out of proportion in our minds.'

'Indeed not,' Denis Peers agreed, as Melanie and Elizabeth turned to leave.

The door leading on to the dirt track at the far end of town was open. With the sun as yet not having risen far above the horizon, there was a deliciously cool breeze winging itself to the schoolroom from the distant river. A pale gibbous moon was reluctant to retreat from a sky that night had already surrendered to day. In the middle distance, the edge of the plain was marked for Mildred Carter by the black-green bristles of gigantic pines. Though she had seen it countless times, Mildred felt a pang of the heart every time she looked at a view that she loved and would never tire of. There was something magical but subliminally savage in these surroundings that even affected the mind of the academic such as she was. At odd times there was a particular kind of sunset here that always, for some reason that she couldn't fathom, profoundly disturbed her.

As she moved around placing a book for the coming day's lesson on each of the small desks, she was startled as a shadow fell across the doorway. Then a man took one step inside the room. She recognized the stranger she had seen in the hotel dining-room, the man who had brought massive fear to the town. Now she was sharing that fear. She tried to pull in a deep breath, but her chest felt too heavy. Her lungs seemed pushed down by a great weight. Sucking air into her lungs, she mentally commanded them to fill up. Holding the air down, she closed her throat so that it couldn't escape, while she struggled to control her terror.

He was not elegantly attired as before, and the gun at his hip was so much a part of him that it turned her cold. Expecting to see on his face a certain earthiness, a pagan grimace, she was surprised when his handsome but hard features changed instantly as he gave her a disarming smile. 'Good morning, ma'am. Please don't be alarmed. I'd appreciate it if you'd allow me just to take a look around for a few minutes.'

'I don't understand,' Mildred stammered.

She was never at ease in the presence of men. That was probably why she was judged so unfairly in comparison with someone like Melanie Larne. Melanie and she were about the same age and both unmarried, yet Mildred was pitied as being doomed to spinsterhood by her plain looks, while the vivacious Melanie was admired as a strong-spirited person who had no need of a man in her life.

'I'm Roscoe Lynx,' he introduced himself, still smiling.

'I know.' Mildred stumbled over her words. 'Mildred Carter.'

Overcome by awkwardness, she held out her right hand, pulled it back self-consciously, then was about to hold it out to him again when he sensed her embarrassment and rescued her by looking away to study the room.

'I'm mighty pleased to meet you, Miss Carter,' he said, placing an almost caressing hand on one of the diminutive desks. 'I really envy you your occupation.'

'Why ever so?' Mildred felt her face growing hot as she wondered if he was fooling with her.

'Because you spend every day with children,' he replied. 'Just standing here in this place of young people makes me feel real good. Children have a magic that we lack. It is the grown-ups who spoil the world, Miss Carter.'

Astonished, Mildred started to speak but ran out of words, 'Really I didn't …'

'You didn't expect someone like me to say something like that,' he remarked good-naturedly.

'It surprises me to hear such sentiments expressed,' Mildred said, more self-assured now because this was her kind of conversation. The men of Rattlesnake Rock reviled this stranger, yet not one of them had his sensitivity. She had to admit that she wouldn't expect it in such a man. She added. 'Our Lord Jesus said that our salvation lies in becoming as children.'

The children began arriving, looking curiously at Lynx as they passed into the room. He said, 'I regret that I missed out on that kind of knowledge, Miss Carter. I have a lot of learning to catch up on and would like to talk more with you. But I must let you get on with your work.'

'Mr Lynx.'

He had reached the doorway when she called his name. Her heart pounded. Her mouth was dry. Unable to believe that she was being so forward,

Mildred told herself to stay quiet. But something was pushing her on, and she heard herself say, 'Are you really serious about learning the sort of things that we touched on lightly when we spoke just now?'

'I really do want to learn, Miss Carter.'

'Well,' she began hesitantly, dreading that she was making a fool of herself, 'when school ends each day I always enjoy a walk in those pines yonder. You are welcome to join me if you would like to talk.'

'I'd really like that, Miss Carter,' he said eagerly. Then a flat expression drifted across his face before the usual hardness came back. 'But you won't do yourself any favours by being seen with me.'

'That sort of thing doesn't matter to me, Mr Roscoe.'

Ready now to take her class, she remained confident enough to turn and smilingly give him a little wave.

The Six-Bar ranch house was a magnificent building set in a secluded area that was covered with tall timber. The house was off limits to all of the ranch hands other than Max Angier, and even he was only occasionally admitted. But with Angier nursing his injured shoulder, necessity had that afternoon forced Major DeWitt to relax his rules. Standing in front of him on the rug the major had proudly imported from the looms of Devon, England, was Howard Emmett, his acting foreman.

'This has to be done secretly but effectively,' the major told the stocky, balding Emmett. 'You live with these men, so you know them better than I do. How sure are you that Bodine is the right man for the job?'

'Let me put it this way, Major,' Emmett said, in his slow way of speaking, 'Bob Bodine is about the most useless cowpuncher I've ever come across, but he sure is deadly with a gun.'

The major scratched his white-haired head. 'Have I got this man right, a little squinty-eyed *hombre*?'

'That's Bodine, Major. He's a right ornery-looking critter, but he's real mean all the way through. The way they tell it he's wanted for two killings in Texas, and that ain't even half the story.'

'Then he'll do,' DeWitt said, with a satisfied nod. 'I don't want him up here at the house, mind you, Emmett. Fix it for me to meet up with him down at the corral in half an hour, and I'll tell him what's wanted of him.'

'Yes, sir.'

'Emmett,' the major barked, and his acting foreman paused before leaving, 'tell Bodine that he'll be finished at the Six-Bar after he's done the job. He'll get a good pay-day, then he rides out.'

'I'll tell him, Major,' Emmett assured his boss.

Leaving the schoolteacher at the little gate in front of her house, Lynx felt really good as he walked back into the main street. Being in her company had been relaxing. He had absorbed every word that she had spoken while they had strolled together through dappled sunlight under the pines. Rewarded by the rapt attention he had paid her impromptu lesson, Mildred Carter had given him an insight on the New

Testament, and had intrigued him with an outline of Plato's *Republic*.

'You've given me a whole new way of seeing things, Miss Carter,' he had said, to pay her a compliment.

'It's never too late to learn, Mr Lynx,' she had told him almost dreamily. 'I have found that with the right kind of knowledge it is possible to live a large part of each day and night inside of oneself. The inner dwelling is far more pleasant and peaceful than the outer world.'

It surprised him that he was able to grasp what she meant, at least partially. Always having been aware that something was missing from inside of him, he now realized what it was. Growing up as a member of an itinerant family, he had missed out on the education on offer from the schools and missions of his day.

Lynx was pondering on how different his life might have been had he received schooling, when he was hailed from across the street. Lon Mackeever, a woman on each arm, was standing smiling at him. The older of the two was the striking woman with whom Lynx had briefly locked glances in the hotel.

'I see you now have two friends in town, Roscoe,' Mackeever grinned. 'Me and the schoolma'am. That's two names the town can cross off your list.'

Holding up a forefinger as he walked towards the lawyer and his female companions, Lynx corrected Mackeever by saying, 'Just one, Mackeever. Miss Carter is under no threat from me.'

'That's exactly the answer I expected from you,' Mackeever laughed. 'I'd like you to meet Miss

Elizabeth Larne, who, come Saturday, will be Mrs Lonroy Mackeever.'

'Pleased to meet you, Miss Elizabeth,' Lynx said as he took the hand of the girl who held herself rigid, unsmiling.

'You've just shaken the hand of the widow-maker, Elizabeth,' Mackeever chuckled, as he introduced the other woman.

Lynx heard Elizabeth's shaky voice plead, 'Please don't say things like that, Lon,' and then he was looking into Melanie's dark eyes. When Mackeever introduced them, she let Lynx take her hand, but greeted him in silence. There was something detached about her. It was as if she was hiding, suppressing some part of herself. Whatever it was, it gave her a mystique that Lynx found compelling.

'Maybe later this evening I'll leave these two ladies to their preparations, Roscoe,' Mackeever said, as they were parting. 'Then we could have another hand of poker together, it you're heading for the Blue Star.'

'I'll likely be there,' Lynx agreed as he walked away, only to stop and turn back when Melanie Larne spoke unexpectedly.

'It's your wedding, Elizabeth, and I probably shouldn't interfere, but as Mr Lynx is a stranger in town I do feel that he should be invited.'

From the sound of the younger sister's voice, Lynx could tell that she was far from in favour of Melanie's suggestion. But, left with no choice, Elizabeth said, 'Of course, how remiss of me. Lon and I would be most honoured if you will attend, Mr Lynx.'

'That's very kind. Thank you,' Lynx accepted the invitation.

Making his way up the street towards the Blue Star saloon, Lynx tried to figure out why Melanie had forced her sister into inviting him as a wedding guest. Maybe she was just bored and wanted the company of a man new to the town. There again, Melanie was obviously extremely intelligent, and it could be that with probably most of the townsfolk attending the wedding, she hoped to discover through observation the identity of the person he had come to town to kill.

Whatever her reason, he was looking forward to spending some time with Melanie at the wedding. Pausing outside of the saloon doors, he pushed all these thoughts from his mind as he made his customary cautious and alert entry.

The saloon wasn't crowded and he had a clear view of the sheriff standing by the bar. Winters beckoned him over, extending a hand when Lynx got to him. 'In a kind of way we met last night, but didn't have a chance to speak. I'm Mike Winters.'

'I guess that I don't need to tell you my name,' Lynx said laconically.

'No.' The sheriff shook his head. 'But I think we should have a talk. Let me buy you a drink.'

'Thanks, you're the second one to buy me a drink since I hit town, Sheriff.'

'Max Angier would have been wiser to have done the same,' Winters remarked wryly as he ordered a whiskey and passed it to Lynx. 'First things first, Lynx. In my job I walk a very narrow line in this town, so though this may not sound important to you, it is important to me. Miss Carter, our schoolteacher, is real good at her job, but she isn't very worldly-wise, and neither is she wise in the ways of men. I'm sure you get my meaning.'

'I understand you, Sheriff.' Lynx took a swallow of his drink. 'News travels fast here. Believe me, I have the greatest respect for Miss Carter, and she'll come to no harm from me.'

'That's how I had it figured.' Winters nodded gravely. 'But you can see my problem, Lynx. You got just about everyone in town streaked. There's Peers, the banker, sitting holding his cards with both hands because he's shaking so much. He's been asking everyone about you, seeking clues as to just who you are after. He's convinced himself that he's the one. I hear Major DeWitt's decided the same thing about himself, and he's running around as mad as a peeled rattler.'

'That's their guilt chasing them, Sheriff, not me.'

'I guess you're right,' Winters agreed. 'Then there's Jake Herbert, who runs this place. He's put a shotgun under the counter for each of his barkeeps, so's they can defend him when you come for him. It gets crazy: Jake's girlfriend, Gabriella Fernandez, hasn't been able to sing a note since you first walked in that door.'

'Me'n Gabriella knew each other way back, Sheriff.' Lynx looked puzzled. 'I can't think why she'd fear me.'

Winters grimaced. 'I can, and there's plenty of others who are just as jittery, Lynx.'

'Whoever it is will find out when the time comes, and it won't matter no more to him then, Sheriff,' Lynx said calmly. 'And you know that I won't involve you.'

Looking doubtful, Winters said, 'I know you won't cause me no bother, Lynx, but you never can tell about other people. What I wanted to say is that just about everyone who you've got worried will be at the wedding of Judge Larne's daughter on Saturday. I'm asking you to stay well clear of that.'

'Sorry to disappoint you, Sheriff.' Lynx shook his head. 'I'm a guest.'

'This is Mackeever's idea of a joke,' Winters said, with a curse.

'It wasn't Mackeever who invited me; the bride did.'

This had Sheriff Mike Winters looking very perturbed.

FOUR

It had been an impressive wedding ceremony. The church was large for a town of that size, and it had been packed to capacity. Supervised by Sheriff Mike Winters, two young boys positioned outside of the church door had collected the guns of every armed guest. The sheriff had explained to everyone that their firearms would be returned to them when the celebrations came to an end. Having anticipated that all guns would be barred, Roscoe Lynx had caused some surprise by leaving his Colt .45 in his hotel room. Many were relieved to discover this, while others were suspicious, fearing that he might be carrying a concealed weapon.

The preacher, a wizened little man, had been rewarded by the unusual solemnity of hard man Lon Mackeever, who seemed to be overawed by the occasion. Though he was a more than willing bridegroom and would make a loyal husband, Lynx knew that men like Mackeever were impossible to tame.

Melanie Larne, standing beside her sister at the altar, had turned her head slightly to look at Lynx, her brow creased in a little furrow. She sent him a message with her eyes that he couldn't decipher. She had a trick of looking away suddenly. Then she was back with him, and the little furrow had become a full-fledged frown.

Puzzled, Lynx tried to hold her gaze. But once again she did her looking away bit. She wore a simple linen dress that was flax-coloured, and had a red rose over her left ear. With her high cheekbones and waist-length black hair pulled back and tied with a ribbon, she could have been an Indian princess rather than the sophisticated daughter of a judge. She stood slim and straight in the sunlight that sifted down like golden dust through the high windows of the church.

Lynx had expected an explanation from her at the reception, but Melanie had sat beside Denis Peers at the meal, quite a way along the table from Lynx.

He was still intrigued now as dusk had begun to blur far horizons while he stood alone in the grounds of Judge Larne's large brick southern colonial home. The cool air out here in the night was a relief for him after the stifling humidity inside. The muted sound of the celebrations going on inside the house came to him where he was standing in the shadows cast by a hedge. Acutely aware of being unarmed, he was wary when a silhouette moved silently across the grass towards him. Lynx relaxed on recognizing Melanie Larne.

51

Moving lightly, as soundless as a cat, she came, looking over her shoulder as if expecting to be followed.

Moving to share the shadows with Lynx, she breathed in deeply the sweet scent of earth that rose from the ground. Starlight dramatically added to her mystique. She spoke distantly, looking away from him into the night. 'I'm a modern woman, Mr Lynx, who speaks directly. Does that worry you?'

'I guess that depends on what you intend to say, Miss Larne.'

She turned, facing him. 'I was looking for you inside, hoping that you would ask me to dance.'

'The idea had occurred to me,' Lynx admitted. 'But you were with a gentleman friend.'

'Denis Peers,' she said, dismissing the banker with a shrug. 'I was just using him to cover my cowardice. I was trying to tell you something in the church, Mr Lynx.'

'Most folk call me Roscoe, Miss Larne,' he said.

'Oh, right, then I'm Melanie,' she nodded, momentarily losing a little of her poise. 'I found it difficult to convey what I wanted to say by just using my eyes. Later I lost my nerve when there was an opportunity to speak to you.'

Assuming that she was worried over his reason for being in Rattlesnake Rock, he said, 'I've been asked to leave a town many times, Melanie.'

'Oh no, you misunderstand,' she said quickly. 'Life here is unbelievably tedious. I have nothing to look forward to other than eventually marrying someone like Denis Peers. I desperately crave excitement.'

'I can't quite figure what you are saying,' an uncomfortable Lynx confessed. It occurred to him that this might be a ploy to discover who he had come to town to get. The alternative was that the dangerous kind of life he led made him a man that some women would follow with a wordless faith. It seemed that Melanie Larne was that kind of woman.

She studied him closely in the poor light. 'I know this will sound terrible and make me appear to be some kind of loose woman, but I would like to share your life, even for the short time you will probably stay here in Rattlesnake Rock.'

'I get your drift now, Melanie, and I understand,' Lynx said. 'But if you mix with me I reckon that the folk around here will run you out of town.'

'If that happened, I'd go willingly, Roscoe,' she said feelingly.

A door of the house opened and the night was momentarily filled with the lively dance music 'Turkey in the Straw', and excited whooping of revellers. The door was quickly closed again but not before a wide beam of light from inside of the house had reached to them, somehow depriving them of a certain colour of intimacy they had enjoyed.

'The kind of life I live isn't one that folk admire,' he warned. 'You'd be risking everything, including your family, Melanie.'

Melanie's shoulders made a faint gesture of resignation. 'My sister took the same risk when she married Lonroy Mackeever today. He's trying to be a respectable member of the community, but Lon's a maverick, Roscoe. One day he'll say *hasta la vista* to the settled life, and Elizabeth will either have to go with him, or remain here in disgrace.'

'But that's …' Lynx began, then said no more. He held his head in a listening attitude. Something, some almost imperceptible sound had disturbed the silence of the night, alerting him. She was about to speak, but he raised a hand to silence her. His ears caught the scampering of a small animal, the flapping of wings as birds flew off. Something had frightened the creatures of the night.

Eyes widening in alarm, she gave a little cry as Lynx suddenly leapt at her. Hitting her on each shoulder with the flat of his hands, he sent her flying backwards. Throwing himself to the ground, he heard her little sigh of shock and discomfort as she landed on the lawn. At the same time, a shot rang out and he heard the swish of a bullet passing above them.

'Melanie,' he hissed urgently. 'Did I hurt you?'

'Not really,' she replied, a tremor in her voice.

'Stay flat, but make your way to that hedge on your left. Get right into the shadow and lie there.'

'What's happening, Roscoe?'

'You're safe if you stay down,' he told her. 'It's someone after me.'

'But you don't have a gun.'

That was something of which he didn't need reminding. It was the thought of being with Melanie that made him attend her sister's wedding unarmed, abandoning a lifetime of caution, of self-preservation. But that wasn't her fault.

Believing that he had heard the door of the house open and close swiftly, he waited. Then his name was called softly, and he recognized Mackeever's voice.

'Lynx?'

'Keep back, Lon.'

'Is Melanie OK?'

'She's fine,' Lynx answered. 'He's somewhere over there in that clump of bushes and he's got us pinned down.'

'You don't have a gun, Roscoe. I'm coming over.'

The wide stretch of Judge Larne's lawn was fully exposed by bright starlight. In a low voice, Lynx cautioned, 'Don't Lon. He'd cut you down before you could take two steps.'

Having warned Mackeever to stay put, Lynx tried to think of a way of getting Melanie and himself out of danger. There wasn't one. If they raised themselves from the ground they would be instant targets. Yet it would be just as perilous to stay there and allow the unseen gunman to creep up on them.

'Roscoe?' Mackeever called guardedly.

'Yes?' Lynx asked.

'Give me a bearing.'

Raising his eyes, Lynx saw that Melanie and he were lying in front of two twisted trees, almost ludicrous in their stance, like petrified dancers. It was a silver birch and a pine curved unnaturally round each other.

'The lovers,' the astute Melanie named the entangled trees in a whisper.

Her voice carried on the night air, and Mackeever called, 'I heard. Get ready, Roscoe.'

Hands pressed against the ground, Lynx tensed in readiness. But he had no idea what Mackeever wanted him to prepare for. Then a grunt of effort from the lawyer was followed by a strange whirring sound. It was made by a six-gun that Mackeever had thrown in a high arc, sending it spinning over and over through the night towards Lynx. Glinting in the starlight, it was coming fast. It put Lynx in a dilemma. If he permitted the gun to land, then he might never find it among the shrubbery in the dark, but if he raised up in an attempt to catch the firearm, then he would be a perfect target for the hidden gunman.

Leaving it to the last moment, Lynx, with supreme faith in his own reflexes, sprung up from the ground. Stretching his right hand high, his fingers stung as he plucked the peacemaker out of the air. At that instant a shot rang out. A bullet tore through the shoulder of his jacket, a burning sensation telling him that the missile had taken skin as well as cloth with it.

Then he dived headfirst to the ground, rolling on his shoulders back in under the hedge. It felt good to have a gun in his hand. His next move would be hazardous, whatever he decided. There was no way he could employ subtle strategy. No room for manoeuvre.

Leaping to his feet, he jumped into the bushes, releasing two shots in the direction he knew the gunman to be. This served to keep the other man's head down, and Lynx was lying flat in the brush before a bullet tore away the dry bark of the fallen tree behind which he was taking cover.

Noting the exact location of the flash made by the gun, Lynx was confident now. Reaching for a short length of branch, he threw it to his right as a diversion. But the noise it made as it landed didn't draw fire from the other man. Surprised by this, Lynx fired at where he had last seen the flash of a gun. Then he rolled quickly away to his left as a bullet passed dangerously close to his head. It had come at a downward angle. The gunman had noiselessly climbed a tree. Lynx knew that he was up against an experienced killer. And he had just three bullets left in the gun Mackeever had thrown him.

As Sheriff Mike Winters came across the lawn with Melanie at his side, there was a concerted sigh of relief from the wedding guests. They had come out of the house to stand together peering into the night. The music had faded away and the celebrations had stumbled to a halt. Sadly, as everyone there was starkly aware, the music would not restart that night. The wedding party had been ended prematurely.

Now Judge Larne went forward to meet his eldest daughter and take her in his arms. He had to restrain himself from asking the question that was on the mind of everyone there – why had Melanie gone off into the night on her own?

'What's happening out there, Mike?' Mackeever asked the sheriff.

'It's hard to tell,' Winters replied. 'Seems like there's only one man, but he's sure got the drop on Lynx.'

'To my reckoning, Roscoe's only got three bullets left. We'd best get out there and back him up, Mike,' Mackeever said anxiously.

The sheriff shook his head. 'We go blundering along in the dark, Lon, and we'll likely put Lynx in danger.'

Seeing the logic in what Winters had said, Mackeever accepted it with a nod. Mildred Carter sidled up to Sheriff Winters shyly and enquired. 'There's been no sound of shooting for a little while, Sheriff. Could that be ominous?'

'There's no way of telling right now, Miss Carter,' Winters advised the schoolteacher in a kindly way.

Filled with anxiety and not having been given the reassurance she had hoped for, Mildred Carter leaned heavily against a marble balustrade.

'Maybe there is,' Mackeever said, looking to where Major DeWitt stood beside Denis Peers. He called to him, 'Do you know who's doing the shooting out there, Major?'

'Lynx is the kind of man who brings trouble on himself,' DeWitt said.

'You didn't answer my question, Major.'

'I have no intention of doing so,' the major declared testily.

'Falling out among ourselves will not help,' Judge Larne said. 'What can be done, Sheriff Winters?'

'Nothing, right now, Judge. Roscoe Lynx is on his own.'

With every muscle in his body relaxed just below the point from where it could spring instantly into action, Roscoe Lynx waited. There was nothing he could do but wait in the hope that the other man might reveal his location. Lynx felt sure that the man had left the tree immediately after having taken a shot at him. Having left the Larne house a long way back now, Lynx could see up ahead the faint lights of buildings at the bottom end of the town. He considered making his careful way there through the brush and the trees. Should he make it, then it would be a more even fight if he drew the hidden gunman out into the light.

Still lying flat, he moved slightly. Expecting to be shot at, he was surprised when the night remained quiet. Trying once more, moving further this time, he again got no reaction from the other man. It occurred to Lynx then that the man gunning for him had left in favour of an opportunity to kill him in some other place at some other time. Taking a gamble, he raised himself up into a crouching position. Nothing happened.

Fairly confident that his theory about the man having left was correct, Lynx stood upright. Six-shooter in hand, he tensed. But the heavy silence among the trees remained intact. Moving in the direction of the street, the undergrowth made it impossible not to make some noise, but Lynx speeded up on finding that he had attracted no reaction.

Reaching a worn path between the trees, he followed and came to a stile that was at the edge of the street. Thrusting the gun in his trouser belt, he vaulted the stile. Landing lightly and noiselessly in the dust of the street, he moved into the shadows cast by the nearest building. There was no one on the street, but it curved sharply up ahead, and the sound of someone hammering came from around the bend.

Keeping to the shadows, he moved towards the corner. Catching the smell of cigar smoke, he pulled in tight to the building and waited. Then he saw smoke exhaled just ahead of him. It came out into the night in a straight stream before expanding into a little cloud and disappearing. The cigar smoker was standing in a doorway, out of sight. If it was the man who had been shooting at him, Lynx couldn't understand why he would want to give his presence away with the cigar smoke.

More smoke was blown out. Reaching inside of his coat to place a hand on the handle of the .45, Lynx asked a low-voice question, 'Who goes there?'

There was no immediate reply, then he heard a laugh. It was a woman's laugh, and then she spoke. 'You didn't want to know me the last time we met, Roscoe Lynx.'

Moving a step closer, Lynx saw a blonde woman leaning with her back against a door jamb, calmly smoking a slim cigar. She was idly looking to where a small man was on one knee in the street, hammering with a stone at a rear wheel of a rickety buckboard. Lynx recognized her as the woman who had tried to start a conversation with him in the Trail's End dining-room.

'Remember me?' she asked mockingly, not turning her head to look at him. 'Rita Duprez?'

Needing information from her now, Lynx came as close to apologizing as he was prepared to go. 'We all make mistakes.'

'You look like a man who's just made another mistake, a real big one,' she remarked, with a tinkling laugh. 'I've been watching you since you came out of the woods along there.'

'How long have you been standing here?'

Drawing on the cigar, she tilted her head back to send a column of smoke up at the night sky, then replied enigmatically, 'Long enough.'

'Did you see someone come out of the woods before me?' Lynx enquired, regretting having snubbed her at their first meeting.

As if reading his mind, she said, 'I'm not one to bear a grudge. Yes, I saw him.'

'Where did he go?' From her manner, Lynx suspected she was lying about not bearing a grudge. But she was the only hope he had of finding the man who had tried to kill him.

'He went thataway,' she answered, indicating the street facing them.

'Thanks,' Lynx said, as she turned to look directly at him.

There was a strangely haunted look in her eyes that both disturbed and alerted him. He was certain that she was about to say something. But she turned away and raised the cigar to her mouth. Pausing a moment, hoping that she would say whatever was on her mind, Lynx was disappointed. She drew on the cigar as if she was alone in the night.

Leaving her, Lynx made his way warily along the

street. Anticipating that his adversary was waiting for him somewhere up ahead, he hugged the buildings to use all the available shadow. Still intent on fixing the wheel of the buckboard, the small man kept hammering away, apparently oblivious to Lynx's approach.

Suspicion made Lynx slow when he was some fifteen feet from the buckboard. Logic warned him that if it were possible for the wheel to be repaired, then it would have been fixed by now. Yet the man was still hammering at it.

Stopping, partly shielded by an upright support of the portico of a building, Lynx watched the man at work. The scene had a completely innocent look to it. Nothing more than a man on his way out of town whose buckboard had let him down. This was someone whom the man Lynx was after would have had to pass by. Deciding to make some enquiries, Lynx stepped down off the boardwalk into the street.

'*Lynx.*'

Rita Duprez's frantic cry of warning came echoing up the street to him, but too late. In a blur of movement so fast that Lynx barely caught it, a gun replaced the stone in the small man's hand. Reaching inside of his jacket for the gun Mackeever had thrown him, Lynx saw the flare from the little man's gun in the darkness, then a bullet thudded into his left side just above the waist knocking him backwards. Colliding with the edge of the boardwalk, Lynx fell face down into the dust of the street.

Head completely clear and feeling no pain, he
rolled up on to his left side and dragged the gun
from his belt. The man who had shot him, an ugly
little creature, was coming confidently towards him.
Still holding his gun, the man was ready to finish
Lynx off if it was necessary.

Letting him come in close, Lynx took great satis-
faction in squeezing the trigger. His bullet ripped
away the small man's jaw. Fired upwards from where
Lynx lay on the ground, the bullet travelled on up.
Lynx watched the misshapen head explode, the hat
flying off and a great chunk of skull and a mess of
brains going with it.

Already dead, the little man took a couple of steps
sideways before crumpling to the ground. By that
time Lynx had started to feel pain. He could feel the
heat and stickiness of blood leaking from his side. A
momentary weakness made him lie back just as Rita
Duprez ran up to drop to her knees beside him in
the dust.

'What have I done?' she groaned tearfully. But
relief registered on her face when Lynx opened his
eyes and looked up at her. She gave thanks wailingly.
'*Gracias, gracias, mucho gracios, Madre de Dios!* I am so
sorry, I should have warned you before, Roscoe. I
knew that was the man. I don't know why I let you
walk into that trap. It was very bad of me. Lie still and
I will fetch the doctor.'

Sitting up, Lynx pushed his gun into belt. 'I don't
need a doctor.' He held a hand out to her. 'Help me
up and I'll make my way back to the hotel.'

Getting him to his feet, needing to support him,

she said, 'You'll never make it to the hotel. Put your arm round my shoulders and we'll get you to my place. I'll fix you up and you can stay the night.'

Doing as she said, Lynx turned to look down at the man with the shattered head as they moved away, asking, 'Who was that little *hombre*, Rita?'

'Bob Bodine,' she replied. 'He's from the Six-Bar ranch, one of Major DeWitt's men.'

FIVE

Sheriff Winters called and had been invited to join
Lynx and Rita Duprez for breakfast in the kitchen
of her house. Having been called out in the night
to arrange the removal of Bodine's body, Winters
had learned where Lynx was and had come to
check on him. Lynx was pleased with how good he
felt. The bullet had passed through the flesh of his
side without doing any real damage. Rita had
expertly plugged the entrance and exit wounds to
staunch the bleeding and had then bandaged him
tightly. Sitting at the table now as a black maid
poured more coffee for him, there was nothing,
not even a soreness, to remind him that he had
been shot.

'Seems to me that you've got yourself a problem
with Major DeWitt, Lynx,' Sheriff Winters said, as he
ate ham and eggs. 'He must have sent Bodine to get
you.'

Sipping coffee, Roscoe Lynx spoke quietly. 'DeWitt may not be the one who brought me to Rattlesnake Rock, Sheriff. The major sent that Bodine *hombre* after me because he's scared. A man can't be blamed for being frightened.'

Across the table from him, Rita Duprez's lips pouted in a dubious expression. 'Surely you can blame a man for paying someone to kill you.'

'That's the way I see it,' the sheriff agreed solemnly with Rita. 'Yours is an admirable way of looking at things, Lynx, but DeWitt isn't a reasonable man. He'll be riled up about what happened to Bodine. Tomorrow's pay-day at the Six-Bar and other ranches around here, which means that the town will be wild tomorrow night.'

'You're saying that the Bar-Six hands might make a move on me?'

'It's likely,' Winters confirmed. 'The major might offer his boys fightin' money.'

'I thought ranchers stopped paying that long ago when there were no more Indians to fight, Sheriff,' Lynx joked.

Winters wryly responded, 'To the good folk of Rattlesnake Rock, Lynx, you are the equivalent of a bunch of marauding Apaches.'

'I won't be causing any trouble, Sheriff.'

'Glad to hear it. I've brought your horse with me,' Winters said. 'You can ride back into town with me.'

Rita Duprez's body seemed to stiffen with a tension of some sort and she drew her hands into tight little fists. 'Roscoe should not be riding anywhere for a day or two, Mike. He was hurt pretty badly.'

'I'll be fine, Rita. Thank you for what you did for me.' Lynx smiled at her. 'And thank you for bringing out my horse, Sheriff. I guess I've got some apologizing to do, if Judge Larne will allow me near his place.'

'Why wouldn't he?' Winters enquired sarcastically. 'You only ruined his youngest girl's wedding, lured his eldest daughter off into the night and almost got her shot, and skeered most of his guests near to death.'

'Maybe the judge will see things my way,' Lynx grinned.

A rider passed slowly along the street outside; the soft beat of the horse's hoofs in the dust was a sound that stirred up a restlessness in Lynx. Draining his coffee cup and standing up, ready to go, he said, 'Thanks again, Rita, I'll never forget you.'

Relaxing, hunching her shoulders in a shrug, Rita Duprez said quietly and unhappily to herself, 'I wish I could believe that.'

Major DeWitt had called the meeting and Jake Herbert had provided a back room at the Blue Star that morning. In addition to DeWitt and Herbert there were three other men present, Clive Wrexham, Denis Peers, and Max Angier. Of the five, only Wrexham the gambler was relaxed. He lounged in a chair, his feet raised on a small table, his face expressionless but amusement in his eyes as he watched the agitated behaviour of the others.

'I'm speaking for a number of people this morning,' DeWitt said, as he paced up and down. 'These are men who are just as worried by Lynx being in town as we are, but who recognized that too big a gathering here this morning would arouse suspicion. They will go along with whatever we decide.'

'I would feel better about this if Lon Mackeever was here,' Denis Peers muttered, swallowing nervously before continuing, 'He would be able to give us valuable legal advice.'

Snorting derisively DeWitt said, 'You don't handle a saddle-tramp like Roscoe Lynx legally, Peers. Anyway, Mackeever's got a mite too friendly with Lynx for the good of this town.'

Peers nodded absently. 'To be perfectly honest, I don't think that I am going to be able to stand this situation much longer. I can't sleep at night, and today I find it impossible to eat. Something has to be done.'

'Me and the major have talked this over,' Angier, his right arm in a sling, spoke up firmly. 'It has to be tomorrow night that it's done. The town will be packed with cowpunchers, there'll be high jinks, arguments and fights, so we can fix Lynx probably without anyone noticing.'

'I want no killing here in the Blue Star,' Jake Herbert protested.

'Nobody's going to get killed,' Major DeWitt rasped. 'We're just going to rough Lynx up and ride him out of Rattlesnake Rock on a rail.'

'You won't manhandle him in my place,' Herbert

warned, before his own temerity frightened him so that his whole body trembled.

'You worry too much, Herbert,' Angier said. 'We'll be fixing Lynx in an alleyway someplace. Fixing him good and proper.'

A grinning Wrexham drawled, 'Rely on Angier, Jake. He's got a whole heap of hatred for Lynx. Not only did Roscoe Lynx get the better of him in your place, but danged if Lynx didn't sleep at Rita Duprez's place last night.'

'That's dangerous kinda talk, Wrexham.' Angier turned threateningly on the gambler.

'I don't see no danger in a man with a busted wing, Angier,' Wrexham chuckled.

'You boys cool down. You'll have the chance to let off steam tomorrow night,' Major DeWitt ordered. 'Like Max said, we're going to put an end to Lynx then. By the time my boys have finished with him he'll never want to see Rattlesnake Rock again.'

In his mocking way, Wrexham asked the major, 'How do you intend to get Lynx alone in a back alley, Major, ask him nicely? Excuse me, Mr Lynx, but would you mind stepping into that dark place so that a gang of my buckaroos can kick blazes out of you?'

'We'll do it, Wrexham. We'll find a way,' DeWitt said, but his lack of confidence was obvious.

Surprisingly, it was Jake Herbert who solved the problem by saying, 'Gabriella!'

'What are you talking about, Herbert?' the major snapped.

'My Gabriella. She knew Lynx way back. If Gabriella asked him to meet her out back, Lynx would be there.'

'Would she do it?' a doubtful Angier enquired.

Giving a couple of affirmative nods, Herbert replied, 'She sure will. Gabriella wants rid of Lynx just as much as we do.'

'Then it's settled,' DeWitt said contentedly. 'You fix for her to meet Lynx tonight, Jake, then leave the rest to us.'

'I can string words together good enough,' Lynx explained, 'but I want to be right for educated folk like Judge Larne and his family.'

He sat on the edge of the heavy table that Mildred Carter used for her desk. The children had gone home for their midday meal, and the two of them had the schoolroom to themselves. Though they were poles apart, their relationship had developed surprisingly well although it was unusual in many ways. Each of them enjoyed the company of the other. Mildred now poured them both a glass of homemade lemonade, before broaching a subject in her shy, roundabout way.

'I know that it wouldn't interest you,' she spoke hesitantly, 'but there's a barn raising at one of the homesteads near here tonight. They are always good fun.'

Aware that she was suggesting that he might accompany her to the local social event, Lynx automatically reacted by becoming distant. But then, realizing that he owed her a lot, he relented.

70

'That does interest me, Mildred,' he said. 'Do you think that I'd be welcome?'

'As my guest you most certainly would,' she replied diffidently.

'Well then, Miss Carter,' he smiled. 'I guess that you and me will be doing some dancing at that fandango tonight.'

Pleased at this, she sat with both elbows on the table holding and reading the letter he had written to Judge Larne on returning to his room at the hotel. Though he had not directly caused it, he felt bad about disrupting the wedding, and also about the danger in which he had, again indirectly, involved the enchanting Melanie. Enjoying the refreshing drink Mildred had given him, Lynx watched her anxiously.

'This is perfect,' she said at last, looking up at him. 'You need no help with this, Roscoe. This is a lovely letter, and I am sure that they will understand.'

'Thank you,' Lynx said gratefully. 'I think I'd better find a boy in town willing to deliver it for a dollar.'

With a sympathetic smile, Mildred agreed. 'I don't think it would be wise for you to go to the house yourself.' She paused to look thoughtfully at the old brown-faced wall clock. 'There is another way. Melanie Larne usually takes lunch to her father at this time of day. Unless I'm very wrong she should be coming back down the street right now.'

The prospect of meeting Melanie again appealed

greatly to Lynx. Thanking Mildred, he took his letter and hurried out of the schoolroom, saying as he went, 'I'll let you know if my apology is accepted.'

'Please do,' Mildred called after him.

Outside he found the street was fairly quiet and he was able to see the distinctive, proud walk of Melanie as she came his way. Several other people crossed the road rather than share a boardwalk with him, but she walked straight up to him. Unsmiling, she said, 'You are a dangerous man to be around, Roscoe Lynx.'

'I did try to warn you,' he excused himself. 'Even so, I am sorry to have put you at risk.'

She smiled then to reveal that her initial stern manner had been false. 'You weren't responsible, I walked into it myself. The word in the town is that you were shot. Did Dr Baron see to your wound?'

'No, Rita Duprez fixed me up real good.'

'That doesn't surprise me,' Melanie said cynically. 'If you had a good reputation, Roscoe, that Duprez woman would have lost it for you.'

Shrugging, Lynx said, 'Then it's as well that I don't have anything to lose.' He held the letter out to her. 'I wrote an apology to your father, Melanie, and hope that you will be kind enough to give it to him.'

'Of course. But don't hold out too much hope. My father is a fair man, but a stickler for the law. He doesn't favour anyone who earns a living in the way that you do.'

'I don't exactly like what he does,' Lynx said

bluntly, aware that he risked angering her.

She gave him a tight smile. 'Believe it or not, I detest my father's profession, too. Does that shock you?'

'You fascinate me, but you could never shock me. I see you as a suppressed rebel.'

'I could be a real rebel with your help.'

'My help would ruin your life,' Lynx told her. 'You are a member of an important family in this town, Melanie. This is where you belong.'

'And where I will eventually die of boredom,' she complained.

'I've always found that what's on the other side of the hill is much the same as what's on this side, Melanie,' Lynx said.

'Maybe so, but I'd like to find that out for myself,' Melanie said, wistfully. Then she enquired, trying to sound casual but the tense way she awaited his answer betrayed her, 'Do you know when you'll be leaving town?'

'My work here is taking longer than I expected. I'd say that I will be staying for a while,' he replied. 'Maybe you could help me there, Melanie. I need to get some money transferred in to Rattlesnake Rock.'

Forehead creasing, she said, 'That's a bit difficult. The facilities here are really primitive.' Then her face brightened. 'Why not try Denis Peers at the bank, he's sure to be able to advise you even if he can't help.'

'He's a real edgy little guy,' Lynx said, with a doubtful shake of his head. 'If I walk into the bank he could die of fright.'

Giggling, Melanie said, 'Then I'd better save his life. I'm calling at the bank on the way home, so I'll mention it. I won't discuss your business, of course. I'll just warn him that you will be coming to see him.'

'That's mighty kind of you, Melanie.'

'That offer doesn't come without strings attached,' she cautioned him with a smile. 'There's a barn raising out at Jem and Gwendoline Edwards' place tonight, and I don't have anyone to escort me.'

About to eagerly agree, Lynx remembered that he had promised to accompany Mildred to the barn raising. Though he desperately wanted to go with Melanie, he would not hurt the sweet-natured schoolteacher by letting her down.

'I would be most proud to escort you,' he said gallantly, but sadly, adding, 'But I have agreed to go with somebody else.'

Mouth tightening, Melanie asked stiffly, 'Rita Duprez, I suppose.'

'Shame on you, Miss Larne,' Lynx exclaimed in pretend horror. 'Think of my reputation! No, my companion this evening will be Rattlesnake Rock's schoolma'am.'

'Mildred Carter,' Melanie exclaimed in disbelief. Frowning and teasing at her lower lip with her teeth, she was staring off into nowhere. 'Then I'll see you there, Roscoe. You will need me to rescue you, I assure you. We'll dance a polka together.'

With that, eyes twinkling, she bade him a cheery farewell. Lynx stood for a while, watching her go down the street.

*

From the window of his office, Sheriff Mike Winters watched Melanie Larne pass by and go into the bank. He had observed her long conversation on the street with Roscoe Lynx, and for a reason that had so far escaped him he was worried about the obvious close-ness of the relationship between the two of them. He was still wondering, and he was sure that he wasn't the only one, why Melanie was out in the night with Lynx at her sister's wedding. The daughter of a judge and a man like Lynx had no common denominator to link them in any way. Maybe he was wrong, and Lynx was simply asking Melanie questions. Several people in town had reported Lynx striking up conversations with them, then making enquiries. Though prudently unspecific, his question had puzzled some, angered others, and worried a major-ity.

Yet Winters felt sure that it was different with Melanie. There was a rapport between her and Lynx that was patently obvious to an onlooker, and disturbing for the sheriff. In comparison, Lynx's inexplicable relationship with Mildred Carter was innocent enough. The only downside to it was the possibility of the naive schoolma'am being emotion-ally hurt. With Lynx and Melanie Larne it was differ-ent. Though he didn't know how or why, Winters believed it could lead to a lot of people getting seri-ously hurt.

Deciding to *accidentally* meet Melanie to ask a few questions of his own, Mike Winters left his office and crossed the street. Going into Wilson's store, he asked for his usual tobacco. As the elderly Ethan Wilson transferred a handful of tobacco from a jar to a triangular paper bag and weighed it on a pair of massive scales, Winters kept an eye on the door of the bank. As Wilson passed him the tobacco and he put a coin on the counter, Melanie came out through the door of the bank.

'Your change, Sheriff,' Ethan Wilson was shouting at him, as he went out of the door, but Winters ignored him.

On the sidewalk, the sheriff adopted a casual pose. Spotting him, a smiling Melanie crossed the street to step up on the boardwalk and remark, 'What is Rattlesnake Rock coming to when the sheriff has to patrol the street at noonday?'

'Nothing to be alarmed about, Melanie.' He laughed with her, patting his top pocket. 'Just been in to buy the makin's, my Bull Durham.'

'And I thought there was going to be some excitement,' she pouted. 'Will you be out at the Edwards' place tonight, Sheriff?'

'I guess so, as the town will be empty. It's tomorrow night that things will be jumping here.'

'Then you should make the most of tonight,' she advised.

'I'll do my best, Melanie,' he smiled. Seizing the opportunity to make his enquiries, he went on, 'I saw you talking with Roscoe Lynx up the street. Is he taking you to the barn raising?

'No, he's taking Mildred Carter,' she replied, looking archly at Winters. 'I do declare, Sheriff, that you are getting around to offering to be my escort.'

Winters saw this as an ideal way to take control of Melanie's relationship with Lynx, and to be around if there was any trouble involving the hired gun. He made a formal little bow, 'I would be most honoured to escort you, Miss Larne.'

In keeping with his amusing show of sophistication, she curtsied, 'Well thank you, kind sir. I accept most willingly.'

Melanie had just risen up from her curtsy when the crack of a pistol shot was startlingly loud on the quiet street. Face white, she gasped, 'That came from the bank, Mike.'

'I know,' Winters answered. Signalling with his hand that she should stay where she was, he ran across the street.

Drawing his .45, Winters kicked open the door of the bank and stood to one side. Nothing happened. Taking a look inside, he then cautiously entered the building. Denis Peers wasn't behind the counter, but otherwise everything seemed to be in order. Moving round the counter, the sheriff slowly opened the door to the office. Then he pushed the door fully open and stepped into the room.

Before him was a dreadful scene. Peers lay slumped face down over his desk, a still smoking gun in his hand. The back of his skull was missing. Blood was splattered over the walls behind him, and messy lumps of glistening brain were on his left shoulder and on the ledgers on the desk beside him.

'Mike?'

Hearing Melanie call from the street door, the sheriff shouted, 'Don't come in, Melanie. Stay where you are.'

Quickly, looking for a note on the desk but not finding one, Winters checked the safe. It was locked. There was no need for further investigation. Denis Peers, a young, successful and wealthy banker had for some reason taken his own life. The sheriff went out of the office, closing the door behind him. A small crowd had gathered at the entrance to the bank, with Melanie in the front row. She was holding herself tight, stiff.

'Has there been a raid, Sheriff Winters?' Len Lawson, the saddler, asked.

'I can't be sure, but I thought I seen two strangers down at the end of town earlier,' a woman said.

'There's been no raid,' Winters announced.

'It's Denis Peers, isn't it?' an ashen-faced Melanie half asked, half guessed.

'Yes.'

'He killed himself,' Melanie whispered, then gave an emphatic nod of agreement with herself.

Old man Wilson put a comforting arm around her shoulders and made a click of disgust with his tongue, 'I'm not surprised, Sheriff. The poor feller's been scared out of his wits ever since that Roscoe Lynx hit town. Denis was certain sure that Lynx was after him.'

'Why should that be, Ethan?' Winters asked.

'Because Peers' bank put up the money for Major DeWitt to buy Jim Cutler's place.'

'But surely the major is more of a—' the sheriff

began, but stopped speaking as Melanie made a choking sound.

'Oh, my God!' she gasped. There was a haunted look in her eyes that went with the tense way she held her shoulders. 'I called in here a little while ago to tell Denis that Roscoe Lynx was coming to see him.'

SIX

Denis Peers' death had cast gloom over the area. The folk gathering at the Edwards' homestead were in no mood for the festivities of a barn raising. The Edwards' house stood on the crest of a low hill. The red wood of the building was so rosy that even the shadows glowingly reflected the fiery sun as it lowered towards far away hills. There was magic in the twilight, but even the glories of nature couldn't lift the sombre mood.

Mike Winters saved the evening. Smartly attired in a well-cut suit of dark material, with an amber tie enhancing his grey flannel shirt, the highly respected sheriff climbed up on to the flat bed of a hay wagon and asked to be heard. The general buzz of conversation first dropped to a murmur then faded into the silence.

'Death, particularly a sudden death,' Winters began, 'brings sadness to a close community like ours. But I think we should consider properly what happened in town today before we permit it to affect this event. Denis Peers died not as a murder victim,

80

not by accident, not through illness. He died
violently at his own hand. He chose not to go on
living. That being so and at the risk of sounding
heartless, I say that we, the living, can choose not to
mourn his passing.'

A murmur of agreement rippled through the
crowd. The sheriff glanced at Roscoe Lynx and
Mildred Carter, who stood side by side at the edge of
the crowd. 'There has been much speculation—'

'Sheriff, I …' A white-haired man took a step
forward.

'Is there something that you want to say, Major
DeWitt?'

Shaking his head, DeWitt stepped back into the
crowd. Staring at the major for a moment, the sheriff then went on, 'As I was saying, there has been
much speculation as to why a young man who apparently had everything to live for, should take his own
life. I do not have the answer, and neither do any of
you, so there is no reason for the question to spoil
this evening. There is some bad feeling, I am aware
of that, but I would remind you that everyone here is
a guest with an equal right to enjoy the evening. If it
should prove necessary I will uphold that right.

'Now, our two fiddlers are ready to start the music,
so I'll jump down and let Jed Edwards come up here
to do the calling for the first dance this evening,
which is a quadrille.'

When the lively music began, Mildred took Lynx's
hand as if it was the most natural thing to do, and
they joined other couples on the level, grassed area
that served as a dance floor. Very conscious of the

weight of his gun in its tied-down holster, Lynx had no regrets about wearing a gunbelt. He didn't intend to be caught unarmed a second time. Melanie Larne who was with Sheriff Winters, was covertly watching him. Lynx was aware, too, of the angry glares he was getting from Max Angier who, still with his arm in a sling, was paired with Rita Duprez. The sun had dropped out of sight some time ago, but it had left a memory of gold where it had set. Evenly spaced flaring torches illuminated the dancers. An aroma of roasting pig filled the air, and as Jed Edwards did the calling and the non-dancers clapped their hands rhythmically, the drear atmosphere of earlier vanished completely.

Mildred was a good dancer but an acute self-consciousness stilted her movements. When the dance ended she stood close to Lynx and said a little breathlessly, 'I don't want you to feel that you have to…'

'Have to what?' Lynx enquired when she didn't complete her sentence.

'To think that you must spend the whole evening with me.' Her eyes went briefly sideways to where Melanie Larne was standing. 'I really enjoyed that dance, but I don't fool myself that I am the best of company.'

'Being with you is a real pleasure, so we'll stay together, Mildred,' Lynx said truthfully.

She squeezed his hand. 'That would make me really happy.'

Despite their agreement, a woman parted them right then. Excusing herself to Lynx, she drew

82

Mildred aside to enquire as to the progress of her child at the school. Waiting, Lynx was looking around him when the fiddlers started to play once more. Laughing couples were moving to the dance area. He looked to Mildred, who was still engrossed in conversation with the anxious parent.

Melanie came up to grab his arm and pull him toward the dancers. 'This is our dance,' she told him with a smile. 'It's time you exchanged education for excitement, Roscoe. It's a waltz, so I'll expect you to hold me tight.'

It was plain to Lynx that she was putting on an act. Her light manner was a façade that couldn't conceal how deeply the trauma in town that day had affected her. Turning worriedly to look in Mildred's direction, he realized that she was unaware of what was happening.

'It's turning out to be a much nicer evening than I had anticipated,' Melanie commented as they danced. 'I was hoping that Elizabeth and Lon would have returned by now. Elizabeth loves this kind of get-together.'

'I have missed seeing Mackeever around town,' Lynx said.

'They were going to Tulsa, but settled for Santa Fe in the end,' Melanie explained. 'By the way, my father responded to your letter with a forgiveness of sorts. Even so, I wouldn't expect an invitation to Sunday tea if I were you. If Lon had his way you'd be a regular dinner guest.'

'Mackeever is my kind of man.'

'He speaks highly of you,' Melanie acknowledged,

as she peered through the crowd to where Mildred now stood alone, looking terribly lonely as she watched the dancers. 'What of you, Roscoe? Do you intend to spend the whole evening with the little school-ma'am? Surely a man such as you needs a woman who can say something other than the two-times-table.'

'Mildred is …' Lynx started to defend the school-teacher, but the atmosphere had changed suddenly, and the music slowed so that it made dancing impossible. There was an unearthly stillness.

Since the waltz had begun, Jed Edwards had been down off the hay wagon to be with his wife and friends. They turned, as did everyone else, to watch Major DeWitt climb up on the wagon and prepare to address the revellers. Two young men, both armed, one with crossed gunbelts and twin .45s, took up position, standing with their backs to the wagon.

'This means trouble,' Melanie said. 'You've got the major really streaked, Roscoe. That doesn't take a lot of doing. My father says that in the old days DeWitt sat up all night holding a Sharps rifle ready to defend his ranch against the Indians. The only thing that's changed is that now he sits up all night holding a Winchester rifle not sure who he should be defending himself against.'

'Who are the two coots protecting him?' Lynx asked.

'I don't know.' A frown laddered Melanie's brow. 'Hired guns I would say.'

Mildred shyly joined them, asking, 'What's going on?'

'I reckon DeWitt is about to spoil the party,' Lynx predicted.

'I do hope not,' Mildred sighed. 'Everyone is so happy.'

A hush fell over the crowd as Major DeWitt raised his voice to begin a speech. 'I'm real sorry to interrupt this fandango, folks, but I won't take up much of your time and what I have to say is important to us all. As we enjoy the hospitality of Jed and Gwendoline Edwards, we mustn't forget that we have a killer in our midst.'

'That's enough, Major,' Sheriff Winters called, as he walked in his cat-like way to the wagon. 'If you can't stay peaceful, then get out of here and take your gunfighters with you. With women and children here this is no place for guns.'

'No place for guns you say, Winters?' DeWitt roared angrily. He pointed to where Lynx stood with Mildred and Melanie. 'It don't seem to bother you none that there's a killer standing there toting a gun. Or are you afeard to face Lynx, Winters?'

'I'm not going to argue with you, Major,' Mike Winters said, as he reached the wagon.

With his thumbs hooked in his crossed gunbelts, one of the men took a half step to confront the sheriff. He was young and dark-skinned with a not unhandsome face, but the coldness in his slanted grey eyes gave everything about him a repelling ugliness. He spoke sneeringly. 'Listen, John Law, Major DeWitt don't want to leave, so why don't you just go back to the women and children, where it's nice and safe.'

Moving closer, crowding the gunslinger, allowing him no room to draw, Winters' left hand grabbed his vest, yanking him forwards. In an explosion of violence, the sheriff's right hand then slapped the man across the face hard, then back handed him even harder. The sounds of the slaps were like two cracks of a whip in the night air. When released, the stunned gunfighter staggered back against the wagon, his lips split and his mouth bloodied.

As Winters tilted his head back to look up at DeWitt, the second gunslinger's hand went down fast for his gun. He was quick, but the sheriff was bewilderingly quicker. He had drawn and his gun was covering the other man before he had cleared leather.

'I'm going to let you live, son, as long as you do it somewhere away from here,' Winters said, holstering his gun. 'You, Major, get down from there *pronto* and make for home.' He pointed at the two gunfighters. 'Take these two with you and send them on their way. I don't want to see either of them around here again.'

The major climbed down from the wagon angrily and stomped off with a gunslinger on either side of him. Sheriff Winters turned to face the assembly, shouting, 'Let's get the show on the road once more, folks. Fiddlers, play us a jaunty tune.'

Within minutes it was as if the dangerous episode hadn't occurred. The music filled the night and the dancers whirled. A military two-step saw Melanie on the arm of the sheriff, but Lynx politely stalled Mildred when she made it plain that she expected them to join the dance.

'Excuse me for a few moments, Mildred,' he said.

Fading into the night, he made his way up the slope towards the Edwards' house. Reaching the summit, he stood and looked east. The moon was hidden behind a veil of summer clouds, but it was a full moon and there was plenty of light for him to see the meandering trail leading away from the home-stead. In the middle distance there was a shadowy, moving silhouette that he could tell was Major DeWitt's buckboard. As Lynx had expected, the two riders who should be accompanying DeWitt were nowhere to be seen.

Lynx went back down the hill. There was no music now. People were filing past the spit where Jed Edwards was slicing off meat that his wife placed on a plate to hand to each guest as they passed. Standing with Mike Winters and Melanie, Mildred held a plate for Lynx.

Thanking her, Lynx took the plate. He spoke to Winters, whom he admired for having handled a potentially serious situation without a shot being fired. 'I guess that my being here caused you that problem, Sheriff, and I'm sorry.'

'The major caused that, not you,' Winters replied easily. 'Do you know either of those two gunslingers, Roscoe?'

With a negative shake of his head, Lynx said, 'I don't know them, but I believe that I've heard of the *hombre* with the two guns. His name is Walter Railkey, and he's building himself quite a reputation down south. I don't reckon he'll take kindly to being slapped, Mike.'

'That's why I slapped him,' the sheriff said, with a shrug of deliberate indifference, although aware that Lynx had signalled a warning to him.

The fiddlers had resumed playing. Melanie squealed with delight as she identified the tune. 'The Juba. Come on, boys, Mildred, let's join in. This will be fun.'

'Do you know the dance, Roscoe?' a concerned Mildred asked.

'Yes.' Lynx was familiar with the popular but complicated Negro dance. He added a warning. 'But I've become out of practice in recent years.'

'It will soon come back to you,' Melanie advised him confidently.

Lynx was thankful that the dance began slowly. He followed the other dancers as they patted their hands on their knees, then clapped their hands together before slapping their right shoulder with their left hand, then the left shoulder with their other hand. As the confidence of the dancers grew, so did the speed of their movements increase. Soon the Juba was in full swing, with the rapidity of the dancers' motions keeping accurate time with their feet, their singing and the music.

They filled the night with their song, creating a wonderfully happy, somehow very special atmosphere. Everyone, including Lynx he was astonished to discover, was filled with regret when the dance ended.

'You were meant for a different sort of life than the one you lead, Roscoe,' Mildred commented with uncharacteristic forwardness.

'Maybe you're right,' Lynx conceded, 'but it's too late to change things now.'

Mildred shook her head sadly. 'Nonsense. You could start a new life right now.'

'I wish that were true,' Lynx was saying as Mike Winters walked up to him.

'For a paid killer, Roscoe,' the sheriff said, 'your social skills are remarkable.'

Lynx countered with a grin. 'As a hard man, Mike, you make a real purty dancer.'

'Don't let that fool you,' Winters cautioned.

'It doesn't and it won't ever,' Lynx assured him seriously.

It was getting late now and the wildly joyous mood of earlier, though still there, was a little jaded. Remarking on this, the sheriff said, 'Melanie and myself are leaving.'

'Me'n Mildred will follow you in,' Lynx said.

But the music was playing, and Mildred pleaded with Lynx. 'One more dance, please.'

'You got your orders, Roscoe,' the sheriff chuckled. 'You'll catch up on the trail.'

Fighting against his better judgement, Lynx reluctantly agreed. He knew that the sheriff was in danger from the two gunfighters. It increased his worry further when a smiling Jed Edwards claimed Mildred for a dance, which delayed their departure.

'You've been abandoned, Roscoe. I know the feeling.'

Turning, Lynx found himself facing a half-joking, half-serious Rita Duprez. He said, 'Sorry, Rita. I have

89

intended to ride out to thank you for helping me.'

'Some women, not me I hasten to add, would say that you owed them a dance, Roscoe.'

Looking exaggeratedly around him, Lynx asked, 'What if that upsets Max Angier?'

'You can always break his other arm,' she laughed, moving close to start dancing with him. She went on, 'I take it the banker wasn't your target, otherwise you'd have left town.'

'He might have been. I'm still working on it,' Lynx answered. Fear for Melanie and the sheriff had built in him alarmingly. He released Rita and walked away.

'Hey!' she called, disappointed and angry as he hurried off through the dancers.

'What is it, Roscoe?' a startled Mildred asked, when Lynx took her by the arm.

'We have to go, right now,' Lynx answered, turning to their host. 'I'm sorry to break in like this, Edwards. I would like to thank you for the nice time we've had.'

Melanie and Winters followed the trail back to town. Only the rumble of the buggy's tyres in the well-worn tracks disturbed the heavy silence of the night. The night birds swooping and diving around them uttered no cries. The full moon was hidden behind the trees that stood along the banks flanking the trail. But there was plenty of light to make the ride a pleasant one.

'What do you make of it all, Mike?' Melanie suddenly enquired. 'How can one man have changed everything about Rattlesnake Rock in such a short time? Denis Peers has killed himself, more than a few people fear for their lives. Even Mildred Carter is lovesick.'

Holding the reins, the sheriff looked straight ahead into the night as he answered. 'Two things I guess, Melanie. One is the kind of man that Lynx is. I don't know what it is about him, but I only know of a few others who were like him. Men such as Bill Hickock, Wes Hardin, and Wyatt Earp.'

'What is the second thing, Mike?'

'The kind of work that he does,' the sheriff replied. 'It's legal and most probably necessary out here in the West, Melanie, but folk don't like it, especially those with reason to fear Roscoe. Don't worry. Things will quickly get back to normal when he leaves.'

'I won't,' Melanie said, so softly that Winters wasn't sure that he had heard aright.

'If you just said what I think you said, Melanie,' the sheriff said, concern on his face as he looked at her, 'you are being mighty foolish. No one, not even a beautiful woman like yourself, could tie down Roscoe Lynx, and you would be real silly to risk everything by trying.'

'I know it's silly, Mike, I'm not in any doubt about that. But I just can't help it'

Their conversation ended there as they rounded a bend to be confronted by the two-gun man from the barn raising. He was standing challengingly in the middle of the road. The sheriff reined up and sat, silently waiting.

'We have a score to settle, John Law,' the

gunslinger drawled. 'Just pass the reins to the lady, then keep your hands high as you climb down.'

Obeying, Winters reached the ground and stood facing the gunman. He said, 'I'm going to lower my hands. If you want to draw, then go ahead and do so, Railkey.'

Also climbing down, Melanie stood anxiously watching and listening.

'You know my name,' Railkey said, very pleased. He shook his head. 'Put down your hands. I won't be pulling on you. I want this to be proper, so's that when you die you'll know that I beat you to the draw fair and square.'

'If it's fair and square, Railkey, then you'll be doing the dying.'

'I don't think so, John Law,' Railkey said confidently. 'Now, first step away from the lady, and then reach for your gun when you feel good and ready.'

Moving silently between the trees on the bank running alongside the road, Lynx took in the tense scene a few feet below him. Warned by a sixth sense that had evolved through long years of experience, he had left Mildred back along the road in the carriage. Sure that there was something wrong up ahead, he had continued on foot to find his suspicion proved correct. Sheriff Winters was standing with his back towards Lynx, facing Walter Railkey. A frightened Melanie stood clinging to the side of the buggy.

A movement on the bank on the opposite side of the trail alerted Lynx. It was too slight and too brief for him to identify it, but it was enough.

He heard Railkey say, 'If you ain't going to draw, John Law, then I reckon that I'll have to push you into it by counting to three.'

'Don't go for your gun, Mike,' Lynx called, startling all three of the people standing on the trail below. 'You've been set up. Railkey's *compadre* is up on the bank over there.'

Hearing a sudden little cry of alarm from Melanie, Lynx was filled with dread as he looked her way. The second gunslinger had slid down the bank to come up behind her. With an arm round her throat he was using Melanie as a shield. Only one of his hands, which was holding a gun, and one side of his face could be seen.

Going down the bank fast, Lynx moved to stand beside the sheriff, who warned him, 'Don't make a move of any kind, Roscoe. What happens to you and me isn't important: Melanie must not be harmed.'

'They'll kill us and then her,' Lynx whispered out of the side of his mouth to Winters.

'What can we do?' the sheriff whispered. 'One of us can get Railkey, but the other guy can gun both of us down and we can't touch him because of Melanie.'

Not prepared to simply give up, Lynx recognized that there was one possibility. If they didn't try, then all three of them were doomed to die. The result would be the same if what he planned to do went wrong. The only difference was that it would then be he who killed Melanie.

'We have to make a move, Mike,' Lynx insisted.

'You draw on Railkey and I'll take care of the other *hombre*.'

'Good God, Lynx!' the sheriff croaked. 'There's only a few inches of the left side of his head showing. That's no target, particularly in this half-light. Think of Melanie.'

'I am thinking of her,' Lynx assured him. That was true. He was praying that Melanie wouldn't struggle, wouldn't move as much as an inch. Her life depended on her not doing so. He spoke urgently. 'Draw on Railkey, Mike. NOW!'

Reacting instinctively, Winters slapped leather. The explosive sound of his six-shooter shattered the silence of the night a fraction before Railkey squeezed the trigger, but at the same time as Lynx fired at the second gunslinger. Railkey's gun thudded as it hit the ground, then he crumpled beside it. Lynx and the sheriff looked anxiously in Melanie's direction.

She and the gunfighter were standing, with his arm still round her neck. As they watched, Melanie's knees gave way and she fell forwards, and the man fell with her. Both filled with dread, Lynx and Winters ran to where the man and woman lay. Pulling the gunslinger off Melanie and on to his back, Lynx released a long, sighing breath of relief as he saw a black hole oozing thick, dark-red blood filling the socket where the man's right eye had once been.

Straightening up from where he had been bending over Melanie, the sheriff said, 'Melanie's all right, Roscoe. She fainted, that's all.' He looked down at the dead gunfighter. 'Well, I'll be danged, Roscoe. I never have seen shooting like that.'

A solemn Lynx murmured, 'It was a fluke, Mike. I got lucky.'

SEVEN

Leaving the hotel just before dawn, Lynx had ridden out to the scene of the previous night's shooting. By the light of a red-tinged dawn oozing over the horizon, he had first located the horses of the two dead men. Then he had dragged the bodies from the undergrowth where he and the sheriff had rolled them a few hours earlier. Throwing each one across the saddle of a horse, he had secured them by lashing their wrists to their ankles. Then he swung up into his saddle and rode off at a steady pace, leading the two horses with their dead riders.

An hour later he rode through the arched entrance to the Six-Bar. As Lynx turned into the yard, Major DeWitt stood waiting for him, flanked by the crippled Max Angier on one side and a stocky, balding man on the other. The stocky man held a shotgun loosely under one arm.

Lynx dismounted. As he put a hand on his belt, the man with the shotgun brought it up to cover Lynx. Ignoring this, Lynx pulled out a knife and walked to the first horse he had been leading. Reaching underneath, he slashed the ropes and tipped the body off the horse. The corpse hit the ground with a thud, sending up a dust cloud. He repeated the exercise with the second body, sensing the scurry of shock that ran through DeWitt, as he turned to face him.

'You wasted your money on that pair, Major.'

'What do you want here, Lynx?'

'Just bringing your rubbish back, Major,' Lynx said. 'A kind of neighbourly gesture.'

DeWitt warned, 'I could have Emmett here blast you with his shotgun.'

'You have two dead men here already, Major. If you want a third, then tell your man to go ahead,' Lynx invited coolly.

The major's skin stretched tightly over his cheekbones, the cords in his neck pressed hard against his collar. 'I'd watch my mouth if I were you, Lynx. You're talking to the only man within a hundred miles who isn't afraid of you.'

'I'm pleased to hear that, Major, as I was hoping you and me could have a talk, man to man,' Lynx said affably.

'What could we have to talk about, Lynx?'

'Maybe you'll want to keep this kind of private, just between us,' Lynx replied, looking first at Angier and then at Emmett.

'Max and Howard are loyal Six-Bar employees. You can speak freely in front of them. I'd trust them both with my life.'

With a shrug, Lynx said, 'It's your life, Major. I

came to Rattlesnake Rock as a friend of Jim Cutler.'

'A friend?' the major sneered his disbelief. Fingering the heavy gold watch chain hung across his waistcoat, he added, 'You're a hired killer, Lynx, and Jim Cutler did the hiring.'

'I'm told that pressure of some kind was put on Cutler, Major, so that he had no option but to sell his place cheap to you.'

'I paid the asking price, Lynx,' DeWitt said, rage reddening his face. 'The way I see it I did Jim Cutler a big favour. He was in some kind of trouble, I'm aware of that. You're talking to the wrong man. Cutler probably had money problems, so you should be talking to—'

'Denis Peers?' Lynx finished DeWitt's sentence for him with an ironic smile at the major's memory lapse. 'That would be a mite difficult now, Major. Anyway, I don't reckon as how the banker had the answer I'm looking for. Jim Cutler knows that he was cheated out of his land, but he isn't rightly sure who was to blame.'

'Like I said, it wasn't me,' the major said, forcefully. 'All I did was to put my name to a bill of sale and pay over good money.'

'Who prepared the bill of sale, Major?'

'You won't get me to tell you that,' DeWitt said agitatedly.

'Then I guess I'll keep digging until I find what I want. Then it's possible that you and me will talk again, Major.'

Eyes narrowing, DeWitt said, 'Maybe you won't be around long enough for that, Lynx.'

'I'm sure I will be,' Lynx said quietly, as he swung up into the saddle.

Pulling the head of his horse round he moved it away at a walk. Behind him, Howard Emmett had the shotgun held loosely under his arm once more, but when the major gestured frantically to him he passed the gun over.

Not a word had been spoken and not the slightest of sounds had been made. But as soon as DeWitt had hold of the shotgun, Lynx stopped and wheeled his horse in a quarter turn. Staying in the saddle, with one hand resting lightly on his right hip, he stared at the major. Both Angier and Emmett took two sideways steps to safely distance themselves from their employer. Finger on the trigger, the major brought up the shotgun so that it was aimed at Lynx's chest. Lynx sat unmoving in the saddle.

For perhaps half a minute, DeWitt, filled with a vibrating excitement, held Lynx's gaze. But then he passed the gun back to Emmett and turned to walk with his shoulders slumped, back towards his house. Watching him go, Lynx pulled on the reins and went slowly on his way.

Sitting up in bed, finishing the breakfast that Melanie had brought her on a tray, Belle Larne's blue eyes twinkled as she slanted a look at her daughter. 'He must be quite a man if he can turn a headstrong young woman like you into a giggly young girl.'

Despite herself, Melanie blushed at her mother's gentle ribbing. In confessing the fascination that the intriguing, enigmatic Roscoe Lynx held for her, Melanie hadn't mentioned the dangerous but thrilling episode on the way home from the barn raising. Both Mike Winters and Roscoe had been magnificent. It had raised Lynx to a god-like status in her mind. Whether she had lived or died had been up to him, and he had risked everything to save her. In retrospect, the moment Roscoe Lynx had fired at the man holding her had been the most exciting in her life. This morning she could understand for the first time what Lon Mackeever had meant when he had said once that the only time a person really lived was when their life was under threat.

'I've not exactly become a giggly girl, Mother,' Melanie protested with a smile. 'I don't really know what it is, but I imagine you felt the same when you met Father.'

Belle Larne's face, its lines deepened by suffering, became serious. 'Perhaps not, Melanie. I loved your father then as I love him now, because he is a kind and considerate man who makes me feel secure. Men such as your Roscoe Lynx are attractive because they are dangerous. I know from experience that it can be quite overwhelming, but neither a long-lasting relationship nor happiness comes with that sort of thing, Melanie.'

Accustomed to knowing her mother as an ageing, sick person, hearing her talk of such things forced Melanie to grasp that she had once been a young girl, most probably a lovely young girl.

'You are giving your secrets away, Mother,' she cautioned with a little laugh.

'I did have my moments, but it was all a very long time ago, and it taught me some valuable lessons,' the older woman confessed. Then she asked plaintively, 'Would you do something for me, Melanie?'

'Of course,' Melanie replied automatically.

'Will you see what you feel for this stranger as nothing but a fleeting infatuation? Please keep away from him. Do you promise?'

Melanie, who would without hesitation do anything in the world for her mother, was ashamed to discover that she couldn't give her the promise that she had requested.

The Blue Star was packed with noisy cowboys, many of them already half-drunk. Lynx eased his way through the throng to where Clive Wrexham sat at his usual table, shuffling cards. The gambler was relaxing before what would later be a hectic and profitable night for him. The only other player at the table now was Lon Mackeever, who made a brief gesture of greeting with his left hand. Then he pointed in turn at three empty chairs round the table.

He laconically identified each of the chairs. 'That's Denis Peers' chair, the chair of a dead man. This one is the chair of Major DeWitt, an absent friend who will probably soon be dead. The third chair is spare. Take your pick, Roscoe.'

Seating himself in the spare chair, Lynx nodded when Wrexham asked him if he wanted to be dealt in. Pushing a clean glass towards Lynx, Mackeever filled it with whiskey from a bottle that stood in the centre of the table. The lawyer explained the presence of the spare glass, 'I was expecting you, *amigo.*'

'I see that you are not letting marriage interfere with your private life,' Lynx remarked sarcastically, as he picked up one by one the cards Wrexham dealt him.

'I got myself a bride, not a jailer, Roscoe,' the lawyer drawled. 'Elizabeth is a very understanding woman.'

'She'll need to be,' Wrexham predicted cryptically.

Adding ten dollars to the pot, Mackeever said, 'Gentlemen should never discuss a lady in a saloon. It isn't the done thing. But at least it stops Lynx asking questions. The way I hear it you've put the injun sign on the major.'

'You heard it wrong, Lon,' Lynx advised.

'Oh no,' Mackeever groaned in mock complaint. 'That means we're going to have more of your darn questions.'

'Only one,' Lynx said softly, deliberately delaying as he observed Mackeever covertly.

'Get it over with,' Mackeever sighed. 'Then we can get on with the game.'

'Did you do the legal paperwork when DeWitt bought Jim Cutler's place?'

Lynx saw the sudden change in Mackeever's face, the sudden flare of his focused eyes, the tightening jaw muscles that widened his mouth. This was revealing in a hard man who was self-schooled in concealing emotions.

'Am I at the top of your list now, Lynx?'

'That's a question, not an answer, Lon.'

'I thought we were buddies.'

'That ain't an answer, either,' Lynx pointed out, folding the fan of cards he held and placing them face down on the table. 'The stakes are too high for me. I'm out.'

Gabriella Fernandez had come out hesitantly on the little stage at the end of the long room, and a hush fell on the crowd. Her chosen song 'When Johnny Comes Marching Home', had a lilt to it that was in keeping with the celebratory mood of the evening. Even the drunks remained silent in awe of her natural singing talent.

Still avoiding Lynx's question, Mackeever said, 'This is the first time she's sung since the night you hit town, Roscoe. She must feel safe, having heard that it's DeWitt you're after.'

'Seems like Denis Peers decided too soon to blow a hole in his head,' Clive Wrexham commented, as Mackeever signalled that he wanted another card.

The song was ending, the bottle on the table was empty, and Lynx said, 'I'll get us another bottle.'

Finding that he had to wait at the crowded, frantically busy bar, Lynx turned, resting his elbows on the counter as he looked around. A saloon girl had interrupted Wrexham and Mackeever's game. With a scarlet smile draped across her face, the girl had dark-brown hair through which glinted strands that had greyed, perhaps too soon. She was leaning close to Mackeever. The lawyer was nodding occasionally as he listened intently to what she had to say. Slender but inelegant, she was wearing a dress of American flag material, combining indecency and patriotism.

Puzzled by Mackeever's obvious interest in sluttish saloon girl, Lynx's pondering was interrupted as Gabriella came up to him. Eyes downcast, she spoke nervously. 'How are you, Roscoe?'

'Surviving,' he replied, paying the barkeep and grasping the neck of the bottle he had purchased.

The smile she gave him was forced. She had good teeth, and her smile brought out dimples that stayed buried most of the time. But things had happened inside of her, under the skin, since he had last seen her up close. This was reflected in her eyes and the set of her mouth, robbing her face of the beauty it had once possessed. Yet she was still compellingly attractive.

'Why haven't you wanted to speak with me?' she asked pensively.

'I understood that you were Jake Herbert's girl now, Gabriella.'

She shook her head almost violently. 'No matter what, I will only ever be your girl, Roscoe.'

'What are you saying?' he asked, her words and the way she looked at him reminding him of the good times they had once shared.

'If you would like,' she said shyly, her Mexican accent very pronounced, 'I could meet you very soon.'

'Where? When?'

She hesitated. 'I have to sing again in a little while. When my song has ended I can go out of the side door and meet you in the alley.'

'I'll be there,' he assured her, as he left her to walk to the gamblers' table.

Taking the bottle, opening it and pouring three drinks, Mackeever asked, 'Have you just crossed that Mex girl off your list, Roscoe?'

'Not exactly,' Lynx answered.

'If you've decided that it's me, Roscoe,' Mackeever said calmly, as he emptied his glass, 'you would be wise to leave it until tomorrow. Tonight you'll need me as a friend.'

'How so?'

'I've been told that DeWitt wants you taken care of tonight. When you leave here for the hotel, don't go without me.'

Understanding now what the saloon girl had been telling the lawyer, Lynx said, 'I've never needed anyone to back me, Lon.'

'You will tonight,' Mackeever warned. 'Good as you are, Roscoe, you are only one man and the major employs a small army. I'm not looking to be your partner. When we leave here, you walk down one side of the street and I'll take the other. That way I can watch your back.'

It made sense. But Lynx, very aware that Gabriella was singing again, had one reservation about Mackeever's suggested arrangement. He said, 'I can't let you do that, Mackeever. Not without knowing whether it was you who drew up the legal papers for the sale of Jim Cutler's place.'

'What cussed difference does that make?'

'Could be that you will save my life tonight and I'll have to kill you tomorrow.'

'Then so be it,' Mackeever said, cryptically.

Men were crowding round the table now and

Wrexham, busy dealing, called to ask Mackeever if he wanted to be in the game. Gabriella had ended her song and, as Mackeever nodded and reached for the cards Wrexham sent sliding across the table, Lynx moved away.

'Where you going, Roscoe?' Mackeever called anxiously after him.

'To relive some memories,' Lynx answered.

'Fine,' the lawyer chuckled, turning his head to look for Gabriella. He added a warning, 'But don't go out into the street.'

Making his way to the doors, Lynx went out and stepped quickly to one side to avoid being backlit by the lamps inside the saloon. He breathed in the cool air deeply. In the dark sky of a new night, a low bright star painted a silver line through a thin mist. With a profound feeling of contentment, he walked to the corner of the saloon and turned left into the dark alleyway.

Eyes growing accustomed to the shadowy dimness, he could see Gabriella up ahead. The Mexican girl stood waiting for him, leaning with her back against the saloon's side door. The sight of her made Lynx quicken his pace, but then a habitual caution made him slow and take notice of his surroundings. All was quiet as he walked deeper into the narrow passage.

As he got closer to the girl, an irregular shadow thrown by a half-hidden moon alerted him. Though still, the shadow had rounded contours that were not in keeping with the sharp-angled buildings on each side of the passageway. Someone lurked up ahead, waiting for him. Stopping, Lynx pulled in tight against the wall.

Waiting for a short while, Lynx then moved on slowly, taking each step with infinite care. When he was within three feet of the shadow some kind of sixth sense must have warned the waiting man of his approach. The shadow took on life and movement, and a figure stepped out in front of Lynx.

It was a heavy-set man, and alarm crossed his square white face. Lynx recognized the man DeWitt had called Emmett that morning. In a swift, trained movement, the man raised a wooden club and held it in a practised stance, ready to defend or attack.

Snaking out with his leg straight from the hip to the heel, Lynx caught Emmett a slamming, tearing kick in the groin with the heel of his boot. Crying out in agony, the man's body jack-knifed forward. Grabbing with both hands the arm that still held the club, Lynx broke the forearm against the corner of the building. It was an expert move, a clean break that snapped the bone like a carrot. The wooden club clattered to the ground. Using the palm of his left hand to push up the man's prominent chin, Lynx drove his right elbow hard into the throat

Coughing and wheezing as he struggled to breathe through his damaged throat, but managing a howl of pain for his broken arm, Lynx's assailant slumped to the dust-covered floor of the alleyway. He lay quivering, with blood trickling from his mouth. Lynx spun round to face two vague figures that came leaping out of the shadows at him. In a split second he noticed that Gabriella was nowhere to be seen. He guessed that she was back inside the saloon.

One of the men started to say, 'Make it easy on yourself, Lynx. Don't fight ba—'

But the man with him was coming in fast and low, arms held high. He was a giant whose snarl broke up his face into a bunch of hard, ugly knots. Stepping forward quickly, Lynx took the huge man by surprise by moving in between his arms. Left arm raised to protect himself, Lynx used the hard edge of his right hand to deliver a hard blow across the bridge of his attacker's nose. With the bone between his eyes smashed, the giant crashed against the wall and slid down it. The alleyway was illuminated enough by moonlight for Lynx to see the man's face leave a thick zigzag smear of dark blood on the wall as he went down. His optical nerve damaged by the blow from Lynx, he was clinging to the wall as if it were a cliff face.

Eyes drawn by the light-coloured material of a sling, Lynx saw Max Angier standing where Gabriella had stood, watching the action from a safe distance. In a short-stepped run, Lynx launched himself at the Six-Bar foreman, who backed off a step. Merciless, a blur of movement, Lynx swiftly and completely dismantled the man with a series of hard blows, using his hands like dull cleavers. Unable to defend himself with one arm, moonlight glistened on a tear that rolled down Angier's cheek. But an impassive Lynx still showed no mercy. Taking one quick step forward he screwed a hard punch deep into the ranch foreman's midriff, who wracked by pain, screamed like a girl. Bending over to catch him by his shoulder as he doubled up, Lynx swung him round, letting the momentum propel him so that he crashed against the wall of the saloon.

Lynx heard Angier being violently sick as he turned to discover that the man who had advised him not to fight back had picked up the wooden club and was advancing on him. The man moved well and looked so capable that Lynx was wary of him as he moved closer.

A noisy eruption of vomit from the man who still clung to the wall hopelessly trying to focus, increased the menace of the man advancing on Lynx. Risking a swift glance sideways to where his buddy lay in danger of choking on his own blood, it was a brief diversion that Lynx took advantage of. His right hand flashed at the hand holding the club. Had it landed, the blow would have broken every bone in the man's wrist. But his reflexes were finely tuned. Moving just enough to evade the slashing hand in a way that sent the now near exhausted Lynx off balance, he jabbed with the heavy club.

Caught hard in the belly, Lynx twisted in pain, reaching for his adversary's head with both hands. Gouging at his eyes with his thumbs, Lynx brought his right knee up fast towards the man's groin. But he was a rough-and-tumble veteran. Though half blinded, he avoided the thrust and Lynx's knee cracked agonizingly against the wall.

His breath sucking in noisily, the man pushed Lynx from him and swung the weapon down hard and fast. Confident of making him miss, Lynx prepared a counter-attack as he side-stepped. But his ankle twisted as his foot stubbed against a stone, and he staggered right into the path of the club, which caught him across the head just above the right ear. After a split second of blinding pain, everything went black for Lynx.

EIGHT

Roscoe Lynx awoke in a room that was warm. Sunshine glowed on the drawn blinds. Though muted, it had a brightness that increased a pounding headache intolerably. Closing his eyes eased the head pain but made him conscious of the agony of his battered body. He had to battle unconsciousness, being so drained that he was likely to slide into deep sleep. Mentally identifying cracked ribs on both sides, he tried opening his eyes just a little so that he was peering through red-edged slits. This resulted in a far more bearable level of pain than before, and he continued the experiment by easing his eyelids up a little at a time. Determined not to relax, he tried to take an interest in his surroundings.

Someone was standing between him and the window. It was a man, who had his back to the bed. Apparently sensing that Lynx had regained

111

consciousness, the man turned. It was Lon Mackeever. Walking over to the bed unhurriedly he looked down on Lynx.

'You sure are one all-fire-tough *hombre*, Roscoe. When I found you, Max Angier and one of his Six-Bar boys were giving you an almighty kicking. Doc Baron gave up on you. He said no man could survive the kind of beating you took. I owe you a drink.'

A jumble of memories put themselves in order and clicked into place in Lynx's mind. Mackeever must have rescued him. This made him argue, 'It has to be me who owes you a drink, Lon.'

'Wrong, Roscoe,' Mackeever grinned. 'I wagered Ed Baron fifty dollars that you'd pull through.'

'You bet on whether I lived or died. Is nothing sacred to you, Lon?' Lynx groaned.

'Probably not,' Mackeever confessed.

'Did you come looking for me?'

Mackeever nodded. 'I knew that you'd gone off with that Mex gal, and when I saw her talking to Jake Herbert a short while afterwards. I figured something was wrong. So I went out to take a look-see. You play rough, Roscoe. You half-killed two of them before the others got you. They'd had enough, and ran off when I turned up. Mike Winters rode out earlier to see DeWitt. As you'd expect, the major denied all knowledge of the attack on you. He said it had to be his cowpokes' own idea to fix you up. Seems like Mike will leave it at that. He told me that no punishment he could give the guys who beat up on you could match what you did to them.'

'Where am I now?' Lynx enquired, looking round the luxuriously furnished room with its blue velvet drapes. He caught a glimpse of someone with a white face looking at him from a mirror on the dressing-table. It took him a while to realize that it was his reflection. It didn't look anything like him.

'Now if this don't beat all,' Mackeever laughed. 'You, Roscoe Lynx, a border ruffian, are a guest in the home of Judge Augustus Larne.'

'Never!' an incredulous Lynx slowly shook his head.

'You can set store to it, Roscoe,' Mackeever assured Lynx. 'Melanie saw me go into that alley and followed me. When she saw the condition you were in she insisted that we brought you here. When that gal gets going full chisel, then the judge knows better than to argue. I'll go tell her that you are able to sit up and take nourishment. She'll be right pleased that you haven't gone coon.'

'I've never been in a town before where everyone doesn't want me dead,' Lynx remarked.

'There's no doubt about Melanie wanting you to pull through, Roscoe,' Mackeever said. 'But I don't allow that the judge feels the same.'

'The judge doesn't interest me, Lon.'

'You would be wise to lose all interest you have in the judge's daughter,' a serious-faced Mackeever advised.

It was a small but determined deputation that stamped heavy-footed into the office of Sheriff Mike Winters. Leading the little committee was an indignant Major DeWitt. Lining up behind him was the blustering self-important town mayor, Oswald Clements, the dour, tall and thin storekeeper Peter Henry, and the prudish Norah Gibbons, who was Rattlesnake Rock's self-appointed guardian of morals. Bringing up the rear was a hesitant, embarrassed-looking Judge Larne.

Standing up from behind his desk, the sheriff asked, 'What can I do for you folks?'

'Just do your job, Sheriff, do your job. That's all that we ask,' the major replied tetchily.

'That's what this town pays me for, Major,' Winters said, 'and I haven't stopped doing it since I pinned on this badge.'

'Except where a certain Roscoe Lynx is concerned,' Peter Henry responded.

'Since Lynx had been in this town he has been sinned against rather than sinned, Peter.'

Folding her fat arms, Norah Gibbons snorted. 'I will take issue with you on that, Sheriff. You seem to forget poor Denis Peers, and that incident last night in which several of the major's employees were grievously hurt.'

'Denis Peers shot himself, Mrs Gibbons, and Major DeWitt's hands were injured because they attacked Lynx and got the worst of it.' Winter's recognized that fear of Lynx had awoken something primitive in his visitors. It made them dangerous in a non-physical kind of way.

'Arguments will get us nowhere, Sheriff, and we haven't come here to argue,' DeWitt said authoritatively, nudging the mayor, obviously prompting him to make a prepared speech.

Noisily clearing his throat, Oswald Clements began. 'We on the Town Council hired you, Sheriff, and we pay your salary. We demand that you either make this man Lynx leave town, or you put him in jail where he can harm no one.'

'On what charge, Mayor Oswald?'

'That is a matter for you, you are the sheriff.'

'As sheriff I work within the law,' Winters said evenly. 'Roscoe Lynx has committed no crime.'

'This isn't a matter of law, it's what the town wants,' DeWitt put in.

'Then the town had better deal with Lynx,' the sheriff retorted. He looked round the others to where the judge stood silently. 'I understand that Lynx is badly hurt and at your place, Judge. Do you go along with what is being proposed here?'

'Well … ahem …' Judge Larne spluttered. 'It is plain that we must not harass a sick man, and I will not permit any guest in my home, even a man such as Lynx, to be threatened. However, having said that, I agree that as soon as Lynx is fit enough to sit in a saddle, then he must be made to leave Rattlesnake Rock.'

'Then someone other than me will have to make him leave,' Mike Winters said firmly.

'We came prepared for such an eventuality, Winters,' DeWitt smirked. 'Judge Larne contacted a man who has cleaned up several railhead towns. You may have heard of him, name of Mart Skelton.'

'I know Skelton,' the sheriff confirmed.

'He's a good man, and he's interested in taking

115

over here as sheriff,' the major said.

'And because I won't do it, you're hoping he'll be interested in saving you from Lynx, Major,' Winters said with a cold smile.

'There's no call to get smart, Winters,' a flush-faced major cautioned. 'Skelton will be riding in tonight. The Town Council has voted democratically, Winters, and if you refuse to resolve the dire Lynx situation, then we'll hire us a new sheriff.'

'Mart Skelton.' Winters gave his head a despairing shake. 'You make Skelton sheriff, Major, and you'll sure as dammit soon have cause for regret.'

'With this Lynx menace rampant in town, we right now regret having made you the sheriff.' Peter Henry put square, yellow teeth on show in a grimace.

'It gives me no pleasure to second that,' Clements said. For all the mayor's bluster there were occasional holes through which the sheriff had often glimpsed a man who was not so sure of himself as he appeared to be.

'So, Winters,' DeWitt began, 'you might as well hand in your badge while we're here.'

The sheriff looked him long and hard in the eye, then moved his head to include the entire group in his glance. 'I will hand in my badge, Major, when and if you make Skelton the sheriff.'

'Does that mean that you are going to give us trouble, Sheriff?' Norah Gibbons asked in her oblique style.

'That would be right uncharitable of me, ma'am,' Winters replied. 'The minute Mart Skelton rides in, Rattlesnake Rock will have more trouble than any town can handle.'

*

'Turn to page eight in your books where we left off yesterday, and read quietly, children. Remember, I will be asking questions later.'

Having given her pupils their instructions, Mildred Carter, unsure of herself and with her face reddening, walked from the front of the class to where Melanie Larne stood waiting just inside the door. The schoolteacher was uncertain whether she was made to feel painfully self-conscious by Melanie's sophistication, or her attractiveness as a female. Deciding that it was probably both, nervousness set her heart pounding.

'Good morning, Miss Larne,' she said, pleased that she didn't sound as inadequate as she felt.

'Good morning. I'd like it if you would call me Melanie. May I address you as Mildred?'

'Of course you may,' Mildred answered, blushing even more deeply. No one had ever shown her much respect, or had ever taken an interest in her. But there was a natural rapport between Melanie and her. Though exchanging few words, they had communicated well with one another. 'What can I do for you?'

'I thought you would like to know that we are look-ing after Roscoe Lynx in our house.'

'I have been terribly worried. How is he?'

'He was very badly hurt,' Melanie reported. 'But he is recovering, slowly. I came here to put your mind at rest. It's obvious to me that you like him.'

'I do, I like him very much,' Mildred confessed.

Emotionally a little off balance, she lowered her eyes. Then she looked up directly at Melanie. 'Forgive me if I am being too forward, but I believe that you have feeling for him, too.'

Melanie nodded. 'That is something that we have in common, Mildred. I always imagined that when one felt this way it would be a joyous thing. But I suppose that we must both perceive it as a cross that each of us has to bear. Sadly, Roscoe Lynx has nothing to offer either of us.'

'I accepted that from the beginning,' the schoolteacher said.

'The one good thing to come out of it is that it doesn't prevent us two from being friends.'

A little ashamed at the ring of gratitude that was easily detectable in her voice, Mildred gasped, 'Do you mean that? I can be your friend, Melanie?'

The children were getting restless, shuffling around at their desks. At a warning look from Mildred, the general buzz of childish conversation dropped to a murmur then faded into silence. Melanie put a hand lightly on the schoolteacher's arm. 'I already regard you as my friend, Mildred. But I must go now and let you continue with your work. I will let you know how things go.'

'Oh thank you, Melanie. Thank you so much.'

It was late morning, and when Mackeever strolled into the Blue Star saloon the only occupants were Jake Herbert behind the bar and Sheriff Mike Winters in front of it. The busy night before had left its stench behind. Mackeever pulled a face of distaste as the reek of stale beer, urine, and unwashed bodies hit him. Mike Winters was toying with a full glass when Mackeever joined him at the counter.

'You dodging the city fathers in here, Mike?' he asked, jocularly.

'No chance of that,' the sheriff grumbled. 'They caught me early this morning, Lon. Major DeWitt did most of the talking. Your father-in-law was with them.'

'Yeah, I know,' Mackeever nodded. 'Elizabeth told me that the judge had agreed to back the others up. She believes that they were going to give you some kind of ultimatum, get rid of Roscoe Lynx or else. Was she right?'

'Exactly.'

'What do you plan to do, Mike?'

'There's nothing I can do. Lynx came here to do a job. He's a professional, Lon, and he won't leave town until he's done what he came to do. I've got no reason to drive him out. DeWitt and the others know that I won't go against Lynx unless he breaks the law, so they're bringing in Mart Skelton to replace me as sheriff.'

'Mart Skelton?' Mackeever mused. 'Most towns get all in a conniption fit when Skelton turns up unexpectedly. Rattlesnake Rock must be the only town in creation to extend an invitation to that sidewinder.'

'They want him to get rid of Roscoe Lynx for them,' the sheriff explained.

'He'll need to move fast. I reckon as how Roscoe

ain't the kind to take to his bed for long,' Mackeever grinned. 'I've taken a sort of liking to Lynx, Mike. If Skelton's after your job, watch yourself. Any time you need a fast gun, just call me.'

'I appreciate that, Lon. But you got your practice to think of. The Town Council pays me to wear this star.'

Mackeever was dismissive of this. 'They don't pay you to get shot in the back by a critter like Skelton. He never works alone, Mike.'

'I know that,' the sheriff nodded. 'I'll be watching him.'

'While you're watching him, Mike, one of his *amigos* will gun you down from in hiding.'

It was late evening and the bedroom was deep in shadow as Melanie, in deference to the sleeping man in the bed, tiptoed to the window. She looked down on a town that was unusually quiet. Deceptively quiet. The idea of violence was present on the semi-deserted streets. Melanie recognized a pattern that was familiar to her. The rhythm of the normal course of life here had been disturbed. Rattlesnake Rock was waiting. Everything seemed to be waiting. Leaving the curtains partially open, she delayed lighting the oil lamp. Turning for a moment, she watched Roscoe Lynx sleep peacefully.

He was recovering faster than anyone had expected. Even so, he was still very weak and suffered intense pain when awake. Carefully, so as not to awaken him, she turned away to stand close to the window. An involuntary shiver jarred down her spine as she saw a rider turn into the far end of the street. The rider came on into town slowly, his horse at a walking pace.

Melanie caught her breath as she sighted three more horsemen some distance behind the single rider. The trio matched the pace of the man up ahead of them. This made it obvious that all four riders were together. The front rider had to be Mart Skelton. Realizing this, Melanie was rigid with apprehension. As a friend of the affable sheriff, she felt that she should warn him. But another part of her cautioned that women often made things worse by involving themselves in the affairs of men.

Sensing that she was being watched from the shadows in the room behind her, she turned her head to see that Lynx was awake.

'What's happening out there, Melanie?' he enquired.

'Nothing,' she stammered.

'You are a poor liar,' he said flatly. 'Tell me.'

Hesitating only for a moment, Melanie realized that Roscoe Lynx had lived with danger for so long that he had developed a sixth sense. There was no point in withholding the truth from him. She explained that the Town Council intended to replace Mike Winters as sheriff that evening.

'And the new man is riding in right now.'

An astonished Melanie knew that he must have deduced this simply by studying her back while she was standing looking out of the window. It was uncanny, and more than a little frightening. Her answer was a whispered, 'Yes.'

'Does the new man have a name, Melanie?'

'Mark Skelton.'

Suddenly sitting upright in bed, pain causing him to wince, Lynx questioned her hoarsely. 'Does Skelton have other men with him?'

'Yes,' she replied, looking out of the window to make sure that all four riders were still coming down the street. 'There are three riders with him.'

'They are some way behind Skelton?'

'Yes. How do you know these things, Roscoe?'

'I know Skelton,' Lynx answered grimly.

Pushing back the bedcovers, he swung his legs so that he was sitting on the edge of the bed. Melanie ran to him as he crashed to the floor after trying to stand up. On all fours, he spoke harshly to her as she grabbed at him, anxious to help him back on to the bed. 'Leave me be. Leave me be.'

She stood back as he gripped the side of the bed with both hands and pulled himself shakily to his feet. Gasping for breath, chest heaving, he pleaded with Melanie, 'Help me to get dressed, please. Then fetch my gunbelt, Melanie.'

'No.' She shook her head vehemently. 'You can't do it, Roscoe. In your condition you'll be dead before you even reach the street.'

'Maybe I will, maybe I won't,' he panted, suppressing a groan of pain. 'One thing's for sure, Melanie: Mike Winters will die if I don't get out there.'

Shocked at this, Melanie supported him, reaching out with one hand for his clothes. She said worriedly, 'I'm not sure that I should be helping you.

The fact that he was too weak to answer increased her doubt.

From where he stood concealed in the opening of the blacksmith's forge, Lon Mackeever watched a rider come out of the darkness of a new night. Unhurried, he came up the deserted main street. The man in the saddle stiffened in alertness as a figure stepped down from the sidewalk to stand in the centre of the street waiting for the rider to approach.

As the horseman reined up, the man standing in front of him spoke. Mackeever instantly recognized the voice of Major DeWitt. 'Mart Skelton?'

'It ain't smart to step out of the night and ask a man questions, mister,' the rider remarked tonelessly.

Annoyed, DeWitt snapped, 'I'm Major DeWitt, goddammit!'

'There's no call to get all riled up, Major,' the rider advised as he dismounted. 'Yes, I'm Skelton. Where's the sheriff's office?'

'Three buildings along on your right, but Winters isn't there. He's up along in the Blue Star saloon. It's best that you brace him there, show Rattlesnake Rock that we mean business.'

'No, Major,' Skelton dismissed the suggestion. 'Saloons are for drinking in, not doing business. You get a message to Mike Winters, tell him I'll be waiting outside of his office.'

Having heard enough, Mackeever moved soundlessly from his hiding place into a passage between two buildings. When certain that the two men in the street wouldn't hear him, he turned off to warn Sheriff Mike Winters.

'I can manage now,' Lynx insisted. 'Leave go, Melanie.'

Having, with great difficulty, helped him to dress and buckle on his gunbelt, Melanie had managed to get Lynx down the stairs and into the hall without anyone in the house hearing them. Now he stood unaided, steadying himself before attempting the walk to the door. His face was as white as a bedsheet. The situation frightened her. Far from fit enough to leave his sickbed, the ridiculously brave but incredibly stupid Roscoe Lynx was heading for gunplay in the night.

Holding her breath, Melanie watched him successfully take one step, and then another. That was when disaster overtook him. The next step made him stagger sideways to crash against a wall. Grabbing at a hat stand to stop himself falling, he slammed to the floor, taking the hat stand with him.

Alerted by the noise, Elizabeth opened a door and looked out into the hall, asking, 'What on earth is happening, Melanie?'

'Sssshhhhuush!' Melanie warned, foolishly, because Lynx had made such a noise when falling. 'It's Roscoe. Please help me get him back up the stairs and into bed.'

She heard the front door close as she spoke. Spinning on her heel, she saw Lynx was no longer lying on the floor. Neither was he in the hall. The curtains covering the glass in the front door were still quivering from where he had closed the door behind him when leaving.

NINE

Sheriff Mike Winters delayed finishing his drink. The tension was there every time a man who lives by the gun has to rise to a challenge. Maybe he had been foolish in rejecting Lon Mackeever's offer of help, but Mackeever had said that Skelton had been alone. The sheriff guessed that Skelton would want to impress the Town Council and would play it straight.

Even so, Winters knew that Skelton was likely to resort to some kind of trickery. He looked around him. Everything was normal. Clive Wrexham had a poker game going, and Gabriella Fernandez was singing a song in her native language. All that was unusual was the absence of Lon Mackeever. When Winters had refused his offer, the lawyer had finished his drink, announced testily that he was going home and walked away.

It was difficult to believe this situation had developed all because of one man, Roscoe Lynx. There had to be a whole heap of guilty consciences in town. Just about every cupboard in Rattlesnake Rock must contain a skeleton. The assault on Lynx had delayed the issue, had prolonged the anxiety.

The time had come to face Skelton. Emptying his glass, the sheriff pushed himself away from the bar and walked resolutely to the door.

'Dear God!' Melanie Larne exclaimed, as in the dark she made out Roscoe Lynx draped over a hitching rail. 'Here he is, Mildred.'

More than half an hour had passed since she had called on the schoolteacher to help her in a search for Lynx. Now, having found him, she was very afraid that the badly injured Lynx could have died from exertion. It was the normally timid Mildred who went to gently lift his head. Lynx groaned and opened his eyes. Melanie rushed to help Mildred get him upright. They both had to support him. When they sat him on the edge of the boardwalk, Lynx stirred slightly, but his head stayed down as he mumbled, 'You women should go home right now.'

'We'll go home,' Melanie said, 'but I'm taking you with me.'

'No,' Lynx objected.

Trying to rise to his feet, he found that he couldn't make it. Taking a small bottle of whiskey from her pocket, Melanie uncorked it and placed it in his hand. 'You've made me into a thief, Roscoe Lynx. I stole that from my father's cabinet for you.'

Gratefully enclosing her hand and the bottle in his, he looked up at Melanie. A hurt Mildred turned quickly away. With Melanie's help he raised the bottle to his mouth and drank deep. He lifted his head and his eyes were clearer when he looked at them. Now with the strength to hit the bottle on his own, he drained it completely.

The liquor had achieved something like a modest resurrection. A new man, Lynx got to his feet and stood unaided. Straightening his clothes, he checked that his gunbelt was hanging right, then eased his .45 up in its holster and let it slide back again.

'I thank you, Melanie, and you, Mildred, for helping me,' Lynx said. 'But you must go.'

'You should be resting in bed,' Melanie protested.

'I couldn't rest,' Lynx said. 'If I do they will shoot the sheriff down like a dog. Mike Winters is too good a man to die.'

'So is Roscoe Lynx,' Melanie whispered, so quietly that he didn't hear her, but Mildred Carter did.

Turning, the two worried women clung to each other as they walked back the way they had come.

Mackeever had reached the deep shadows of the porticoes of the Wells Fargo building unnoticed. An occasional slight movement outside of the sheriff's office that told him Mart Skelton was waiting there.

Seeing someone come out of the Blue Star saloon far up the street, Mackeever recognized the lithe walk of Mike Winters. He wondered what position he should take up to best help Winters. The sheriff was a proud man. His pride prevented him from carrying a rifle, and he would never go for his gun until the man he was facing slapped leather.

That pride could get him killed if, as was likely, the concealed Skelton was already holding a gun on the sheriff. All that Skelton need do was make a slight noise, just enough to have Winters go for his gun. Skelton could then pull the trigger and it would look as if he had beaten the sheriff to the draw.

Mackeever decided he must move closer to Skelton. He planned his moves. The shadowy walkway outside Rob Hayley's general store across the street would get him two-thirds of the way to Skelton. Ready to move, Mackeever was startled to hear his name called in a hoarse whisper.

'Mackeever.'

The disembodied voice had come out of the dark to his right. Hand going to the handle of his holstered gun, Mackeever hissed 'Who goes there?'

'Lynx.'

'Landsakes, Roscoe!' Mackeever exclaimed in a terse whisper. 'You haven't got the strength to sit upright, *amigo*, so stay out of this. I can handle it. I'm going across the street.'

'No!' Lynx spoke the one word so sharply that it sounded terribly loud in the night. His voice returned to a whisper. 'There's a *hombre* with a rifle on the balcony of the general store, and another with a rifle across the street from where Skelton's waiting.

'Skelton has two men with him?' Mackeever half-asked, incredulously.

'Three,' Lynx corrected him. 'There's one inside the sheriff's office.'

Lowering her voice so that her invalid mother wouldn't hear, Melanie pleaded with her father. 'You have to stop it. Sheriff Winters has been good to this town and he deserves our support.'

'It is a Town Council decision. They won't listen to one man.'

'You are a judge, Father,' Melanie reminded him. She was unable to understand his reluctance to ensure that justice was done. It was wholly out of character. 'Major DeWitt and the others will listen to you. They will do as you say.'

Shaking his head, the judge said, 'No, Melanie. Had the sheriff done what the council asked of him and run this Lynx fellow out of town, then this would not be happening.'

'But Lynx is out there now, dead on his feet, but determined to help Mike Winters,' Melanie protested. 'He knows that what the council intends doing is wrong.'

'I gave Lynx hospitality, but I will not help that man in any other way, Melanie.'

'Then what of Lon?' Melanie retorted. 'Lon Mackeever, your son-in-law. He's out there on the street, too, Father. Ready to risk his life to protect Sheriff Winters.'

'Lon must do as he wishes,' Judge Larne replied. 'It must not be forgotten that Lynx came to Rattlesnake Rock with the express purpose of killing a man.'

Aware of the intrigue of politics, a nod here and a wink there, Melanie accepted that her father had no alternative at times but to go along with slightly dubious Town Council decisions. But never would he tolerate unfairness or corruption. This prompted her to ask, 'You won't do anything to help Sheriff Winters, Father?'

'I *can't* do anything to help the sheriff, Melanie,' he replied tiredly.

Afraid that he was losing his fight against exhaustion that was exacerbated by pain, Lynx leaned his back against a door. He summoned enough strength to call softly to Mackeever, 'We need to make a move so as to warn the sheriff before he walks into the trap.'

'That's for sure, but how?' Mackeever asked. 'Can you see the bushwhacker up on the balcony across the street, Roscoe?'

'No, he's crouching up there. But we have to get him first.' Lynx paused to gain the strength to continue talking. 'If you step out, he'll have to stand up to take a shot at you.'

Mackeever was sceptical. 'And you'll get him. You're good, Roscoe, but you were more dead than alive last time I saw you, and you can't have improved much since.'

'I'm alive,' Lynx assured him. 'Just do it, Lon.'

'Now!' Mackeever said, after a short moment of hesitation, and stepped out.

As a shadowy figure, a rifle to its shoulder, stood up on the balcony, Lynx pushed himself away from the door and raised his six-gun. The effort brought on an attack of giddiness that disabled him. There was three or four Lon Mackeevers in front of him, each one slightly offset from the other, all of them spinning wildly. Unable to correct his vision, anxious about Mackeever, he leaned back against the wall for support, but was so weak that he slid down into a crumpled heap on the sidewalk. Lying there, helpless, he heard two shots in quick succession.

With the giddiness receding as quickly as it had occurred, he lifted his .45 as the dark figure of a man approached him cautiously. The man came close to stand looking down at him. Lynx heard Mackeever's voice say cynically, 'Lower your gun, Roscoe. It's too late to help me now.'

'Lon! Thank God!'

'You owe me a pair of boots, Roscoe. I managed to get that *hombre* just as he fired.' Mackeever held his right foot in front of Lynx's face. 'His bullet took half the heel clean away.'

'I'll buy you a pair tomorrow,' Lynx promised. 'Help me up.'

'What's the point? You'll only fall straight down again.'

Lynx shook his head. 'No. It only hits me occasionally, Lon. I could have got you shot.'

'No, Roscoe. I owe you for warning me,' Mackeever said, as he pulled Lynx up on to his feet. 'The sheriff will have taken cover on hearing the shots. But Skelton will move in on him.'

'Then we'd better get moving, Lon. You take the other side of the street, I'll stay on this side. You watch for the man on the roof this side and I'll look out for Skelton and his sidekick.'

'Do you think you can make it?' Mackeever asked, as he started to cross the street.

'I'll make it,' Lynx replied with a confidence that he didn't feel.

They moved up the street in parallel and slowly.

The sound up ahead of a door being opened cautiously had Lynx signal to Mackeever before stopping in the first available shadow. The door hinges creaked again. Lynx moved fast.

Taking three quick steps, he reached the partially open door and hit it with his shoulder. With his left hand he grabbed the person who had opened the door. The flesh of the arm he held was soft. There was a squeal as he jabbed the muzzle of his six-gun hard into the figure, and he breathed in the fragrance of expensive perfume.

'Go easy, Roscoe, I'm on your side,' a female voice complained.

It was Rita Duprez, and Lynx asked tersely, 'Rita! What are you doing here?'

'Looking after my interests,' she answered calmly. 'Sheriff Winters gives me no bother with my business. I'll do whatever is necessary to keep things the way they are.'

It was too glib an answer. Lynx told her, 'Mackeever and me are taking care of things.'

''What was the shooting?' she asked.

'Mackeever got one of Skelton's men,' Lynx said. 'I'm moving on now, so close this door and keep it shut, Rita.'

'No, Roscoe.' She was adamant. 'This is really about you, not the sheriff. The Town Council plan to have you gunned down in the shoot-out. That way Skelton will get the blame.'

'How do you know this?'

Impatient at Lynx's doubt, Rita Duprez replied, 'Max Angier told me. The major's got him up there

133

waiting to get you while you and Mackeever are helping Mike Winters.'

'Where will Angier be, Rita?' a grateful Lynx asked.

'I don't know, Roscoe. He didn't say,' she replied anxiously.

Showing his gratitude by placing a hand on her shoulder, Lynx said, 'Thank you, Rita. You chose to betray Angier to save me.'

'It was an easy choice, Roscoe,' she said meaningfully, as he went out of the door.

Outside again, Lynx signalled to the waiting Mackeever. They started up the street once more at the same cautious pace as before. Max Angier's presence added a dangerous dimension to the situation. Neither was it certain that Skelton and his remaining two men were still in the same positions. The earlier shooting would mean that Mackeever and himself would be expected.

Though thankful that he'd had no more dizzy spells, Lynx became increasingly aware of what every movement cost him in pain and fatigue. A rifle shot split the night air. He heard Mackeever hit the board-walk across the street. From the way Mackeever had gone down, Lynx judged that he hadn't been hit but had taken evasive action. He checked his theory.

'Mackeever?'

'I'm OK, Roscoe,' Mackeever called back guardedly. 'But he's got me pinned down. He's just along from you in an upper floor window of the old Buckaroo saloon.'

Lynx knew the semi-derelict building. He had

heard that the Buckaroo, unable to stand the competition, had closed down when Jake Herbert had arrived in Rattlesnake Rock to open his hugely popular Blue Star Saloon. With the sharpshooter inside the building there was no way of getting him from the street. Lynx would have to go in after him. It had to be done quickly if they were going to help Sheriff Winters. The rifle spoke again.

The fact that the bullet hadn't come in his direction had Mackeever call out urgently but in a low voice, 'He's got Mike Winters pinned down, too, Roscoe. He's got the sheriff trapped like a bogged cow, which means Skelton and the other *hombre* will have no problem moving in and finishing Mike off.'

It was now essential to get the man with the rifle immediately. Lynx warned Mackeever. 'There are three of them, Lon. Max Angier is mixed in with this, too.'

Mackeever answered this with a one-word curse. Then Lynx whispered across the street that he was going into the old saloon. Moving along tight against a building, he came to the dark gap between it and the defunct Buckaroo. Remembering that the front of the saloon was boarded up, he went into the darkness of the alley, feeling along the wall as he went. His hand came to rest against a door, which gave a little. Lynx entered.

In the dim light of the interior he could see that everything was in a state of neglect. Drawing his .45, Lynx moved carefully towards a narrow staircase on his left. With one foot he gently tested the bottom stair. It didn't creak. Encouraged, he made his way up, one cautious step at a time. The fifth step first objected to his weight with a groan, and then a sharp cracking sound.

A scuffling sound came from above, and then a man appeared at the top of the stairs, holding a rifle that was aimed down at Lynx. Lynx blinked rapidly as the figure above him became blurred. Then his surroundings began to spin, fast. Trying to stay upright, Lynx unknowingly leaned to his right. The banister rail beside him broke away under his weight.

With nothing to support him, Lynx fell sideways off the stairs to crash to the floor on his back. His already damaged body reacted agonizingly to the heavy fall. Knocked from his hand by the impact, his .45 went skidding across the floor to come to rest far from his reach. Yet the fall had cleared Lynx's giddiness. Paralysed by pain, he saw the rifleman come part way down the stairs to stand and look down at him.

He was not young, but he had the kind of lean, loose-limbed build of a particular kind of fighting man with formidable lightning reflexes and fast movements. Lynx waited resignedly, anticipating a bullet but able to do nothing to avoid being shot.

But the other man obviously didn't want to reveal his location to anyone outside by firing a shot. Descending to the third stair, he held his rifle by the barrel and rammed it down with the intention of crushing Lynx's skull with the butt.

Life and movement returned to Lynx suddenly and unexpectedly. Reaching up, he grabbed the stock of the rifle and pulled hard. Taken by surprise the man on the stairs lost his balance and toppled forwards. But he was determined not to release his rifle. Lynx tugged again, unwittingly pulling the man down on to the sharp end of one of the splintered banister uprights. Mouth and eyes opening in a silent scream, the man was impaled, the stake entering his chest and coming out of his back in a spurting fountain of blood.

Leaving him gasping his last breaths, squirming on the stake, legs kicking, Lynx took the rifle, picked up his own handgun, and went out of the building. He went unsteadily across the street to where Mackeever waited.

Seeing that Lynx was now in possession of a rifle, Mackeever remarked admiringly, 'You sure deserve the reputation you've got, Roscoe.'

Lynx said, 'Let's get them. They don't know we've got their man in the Buckaroo.'

This was proved true when they saw Skelton ahead of them. He was standing unafraid in the centre of the street, level with the sheriff's office, shouting, 'Show yourself, Winters. We can settle this, man to man.'

There was no movement, nothing but silence as Skelton's challenge died on the night air. Then Lynx tensed and heard Mackeever's sharp intake of breath as Sheriff Winters appeared further up the street. The sheriff strolled almost leisurely to the middle of the street to face Skelton. Winters stood with his right hand held still above his holstered gun.

'Goddamn Mike Winters and his goddamn pride,' Mackeever muttered.

Bringing his rifle to cover the doorway of the sheriff's office, Lynx whispered out of the side of his mouth, 'I've got Skelton's man covered, Lon.'

He heard the sheriff's voice saying, 'I'm waiting, Skelton. Make your move whenever you're ready.'

Things happened rapidly then. Lynx's rifle blasted at a movement in the doorway of the sheriff's office. There was the sound of a body hitting the boards hard. Aware that he was on his own, Mart Skelton turned, intending to flee from Mike Winters, but Mackeever stopped him.

'Stay where you are and face the sheriff, Skelton,' the lawyer ordered. 'I've got you covered and I'll blast you to kingdom come if you try to run.'

With the courage of a cornered rat, Skelton turned to face Winters again. He went for his gun with a speed that would put many a top gunslinger to shame. But Mike Winters shaded him. His bullet spun Skelton round before he had chance to fire a shot. Skelton fell dead and only the distant echo of the sheriff's gunshot disturbed the new quiet of the night.

Relieved that it was all over, Lynx leaned weakly against Mackeever. If the lawyer hadn't supported him he would have collapsed on to the dusty street. But a momentary glint of moonlight on steel a little further up the street alerted him. Realizing that Mackeever and he had forgotten Max Angier, Lynx knew that Major DeWitt's foreman had Sheriff Winters in his sights. There was no time to fire a shot at Angier. Given strength and energy by the urgency of the situation, Lynx let his rifle fall to the ground.

Sprinting to where Winters stood looking down at Skelton, Lynx dived at the sheriff. His shoulder slammed into Winter's midriff, knocking him off his feet. Just as the two of them went crashing to the ground, a bullet whistled by inches above them.

The sheriff quickly got to his feet, but Lynx lay inert in the dust. Mackeever had picked up the rifle and had the shadow that was Angier in his sights. But he was distracted by a woman's scream.

'*Roscoe!*'

Rita Duprez came running wildly up the street, and Mackeever had to lower the rifle as she came between him and Angier, his target. Sobbing, she dropped to her knees beside Lynx.

'He hasn't been hit, Rita,' the sheriff assured her. 'He's still suffering from that beating that he took.'

She was smoothing Lynx's hair back from his face when another shot rang out. Not making a sound, Rita Duprez flopped across Lynx. As if he'd been asleep and she had awoken him, Lynx came round. Gently easing her weight from him, he got up from the ground just as Max Angier came running up.

Both the Sheriff and Mackeever had Angier covered, but he knelt and took the body of Rita Duprez in his arms. Cuddling her to him, he rocked back and forth, crying, 'Rita! Rita! What have I done?'

Knocking Angier's hat off, an angry Lynx grabbed him by the hair to pull him up to his feet. He hissed, 'You're wearing a gun, Angier. Step back aways and draw it.'

Visibly trembling, Angier dropped back on to his

knees and held the dead woman to him again. With a look of disgust at the weeping man, Lynx turned and walked away. He had taken only a few steps when he started reeling.

'Take care of Roscoe, Lon,' Sheriff Winters said. 'I'll lock up Angier and then make arrangements for poor Rita.'

Running after Lynx, Mackeever caught him as he was about to collapse.

TEN

The morning was oppressive with a grey sky. It affected the meeting in the courthouse. Major DeWitt was angry addressing a gloomy gathering.

'In spite of last night's needless killings, gentlemen, we still have a sheriff who refuses to do our bidding, while Roscoe Lynx is residing once again in your house, Judge Larne.'

The judge shifted uncomfortably in his chair, unable to answer the accusation. Lon Mackeever spoke up to rescue his beleaguered father-in-law. 'That is true, but the judge had nothing whatsoever to do with Lynx being taken to his house last night. That happened through the kindness and compassion of Miss Melanie Larne. Lynx needed urgent medical attention.'

When Mackeever sat back down, Sheriff Winters pointed a finger at DeWitt. 'You referred to unnecessary killing last night, Major DeWitt. We should grieve over only one death: that is the murder of Miss

141

Rita Duprez by Max Angier, your ranch foreman, Major.'

An embarrassed DeWitt remained silent, and it was Oswald Clements, the town mayor who said, 'Could you outline the present situation for us please, Sheriff?'

'I'm holding Angier in jail until Judge Larne can give a date for his trial.'

Peter Henry, who wore an apron, having come straight from his store, cleared his throat. 'I believe that Mr Clements was enquiring about the present situation regarding Lynx, Sheriff.'

'That was made clear earlier,' Sheriff Winters replied. 'Roscoe Lynx is recuperating at Judge Larne's house. He should be fit in a few days.'

'And what then, Sheriff?' Norah Gibbons enquired. 'Can we expect him to leave?'

'I would remind you, Miss Gibbons, and everyone here,' Mackeever broke into the conversation, 'That last night Roscoe Lynx saved the lives of Sheriff Winters and myself.'

With an indignant snort, Norah Gibbons said, 'And I would remind you, Mr Mackeever, that Lynx came to the town to take a life.'

'That's his business, not ours,' Mackeever retorted.

'On the contrary,' Major DeWitt argued. 'It concerns all of us.'

'That is very true,' Mayor Clements agreed. 'We rely on you to deal with Lynx, Sheriff.'

'If Lynx breaks the law, then I will deal with him,' the sheriff said.

Norah Gibbons announced primly, 'I am afraid that is not good enough, Sheriff.'

'I'm sorry to hear that, Miss Gibbons,' Mike Winters said as he stood and walked out.

'How is he?'

Arms full of shopping, Melanie Larne stopped to answer Mildred Carter's question. 'He's recovering fast. He's up and about this morning. My father is out of town today, so I've settled Roscoe down in his study. Why don't you call to see him, Mildred?'

Facing flushing, Mildred stammered, 'I really couldn't. I would feel so awkward.'

'There's no reason why you should. I know Roscoe would be pleased to see you.'

'Well, perhaps I will call in some time later,' Mildred said unconvincingly.

Saying a friendly farewell, Melanie knew that Mildred would never find the courage to call on Roscoe. This made her wonder about the immediate future. What would happen when Lynx was fit to do the job that had brought him to Rattlesnake Rock? The natural rapport between them had changed into something more substantial. He would be unable to stay, so what sort of future did that leave for her? There was no chance that another man like Roscoe Lynx would ever come riding into town. That left the years ahead looking very bleak. She could be destined to be an old maid.

Reaching the house, she decided to live for the moment. Roscoe was waiting for her. Placing her purchases on a table, she glanced through the glass door into her father's study. She was surprised to see that Lynx was standing, hastily closing a drawer in the judge's sturdy desk. When she opened the door and entered the room he was sitting in a chair by the window, greeting her with a smile.

Sheriff Winters was moodily resting with both elbows on the Blue Star bar when Mackeever walked up to him. 'It hasn't got any better, Mike. Look at Jake, as jumpy as a fresh-branded calf.'

'He's like those good citizens we just left at the courthouse, each one of them expecting to feel the muzzle of Lynx's Colt jabbing them in the ribs at any time,' the sheriff complained.

Buying them both a drink, Mackeever raised his glass. 'Here's to Roscoe Lynx. Whoever it is he's after, I'll be sorry when he finds him. I've kinda got used to having Roscoe around.'

'I feel the same way,' the sheriff admitted. 'But what if you're his man, Lon?'

'Then I'll be even sorrier,' Mackeever grinned.

'And probably dead,' Winters predicted.

'That too,' Mackeever agreed. 'Come on, get the drinks in. You'll have me as nervous as Jake and the others if we keep this conversation going.'

Ordering two more drinks, the sheriff asked, 'Who do you think it could be, Lon?'

'My money was on DeWitt,' Mackeever replied, 'but I've changed my mind. Right now I wouldn't even try to guess who it is.'

*

Melanie knew that time was short. Her father had been sitting at a court in a neighbouring town, was due to arrive home shortly. Curious as to why Lynx had been going through a drawer of her father's desk, she had decided to investigate. After taking tea up to her mother in the bedroom, she made her way furtively into the judge's study.

Going to the desk, she took out a heavy, red-covered ledger that was simply a record of court proceedings. Placing it on the desk, she took out a handful of papers. They were to do with the upkeep of the courthouse. Next was a list of Town Council members and a record of meetings. For some reason Melanie's heart skipped a beat as she picked up a legal document.

It was a deed drawn up by her father covering the sale of Jim Cutler's ranch to Major DeWitt. Melanie had a fair knowledge of legal matters, and she immediately recognized the flaws in the deed. Jim Cutler had been cheated abominably.

Someone came to stand in the study doorway. Hastily trying to cram the documents and ledger back into the drawer, she realized it was not her father but Roscoe Lynx. Equally as uncomfortable as Melanie was, he spoke in a gentle voice. 'Thank you for all that you have done for me, Melanie, but now I think it best that I go back to stay in the hotel.'

'You know, don't you,' she said, using her eyes to indicate the deed.

He nodded, murmured, 'I am really sorry, Melanie,' and turned to walk away.

The truth of the situation hit her. Lynx had learned that her father was the man he had come to Rattlesnake Rock to kill. Her first thought was for her mother. Without her loving and attentive husband, the invalid Belle Larne would fade away in no more than a few weeks. Melanie probably wouldn't survive herself without her doting father. It would be hard on Elizabeth, too, but she had a husband now.

Ready to beg Lynx to spare her father, she ran to call after him. 'Roscoe!'

Not slowing his pace or turning his head, Lynx continued on his way down the street.

Stiff in the joints after what was a fairly short ride, Judge Larne dismounted and passed a silver coin to a stable lad. 'See that he is properly groomed, fed and watered, Jeremiah.'

'Yes, Judge Larne,' the boy said, unhitching the judge's canvas bag from the saddle.

Placing the bag under one arm, the judge walked out into the poor light of a dull evening. His day had gone reasonably well, allowing him time to purchase a small gift for his wife. The judge knew how much it meant to her to have him bring home some special little present each time he was out of town. Envisaging her delight, he was smiling to himself when he came to an abrupt halt. Until the last moment he hadn't noticed that a man was standing directly in his path.

'Judge Larne,' the man said, making it a statement and not a question.

'Lynx,' the judge said affably. Then he saw the expression on Lynx's face, and he felt suddenly faint. Taking a handkerchief from his pocket he dabbed at his nose. The cotton was instantly stained red. He asked, 'Does this mean what I think it means?'

'I'm afraid so, Judge.'

'I am not a coward, Lynx, but I would earnestly ask you not to distress my family. You do what you have to do, but not at my home. How long do I have?'

Pausing before his reply, Lynx said, 'I won't trouble you at your house, sir. Perhaps we could meet somewhere to discuss this tomorrow evening.'

'That would be most suitable for me,' the judge answered. 'Do you know the recreation field at the end of town?'

'I know it.'

'Very well. I will be there at seven o'clock tomorrow evening.'

As Judge Larne was hurrying away, Lynx called after him, 'Judge.'

Stopping, the judge turned.

'Be sure to come armed,' Lynx said.

The news was all over the town the next morning. Mildred Carter had difficulty in believing it until she asked a distraught Melanie Larne. Mildred, close to tears, held her friend's hands. 'This is terrible, Melanie. I think if I talk to Roscoe I'll be able to persuade him to spare your father.'

Shaking her head, Melanie said, 'That is sweet and

147

kind of you, Mildred, but Roscoe Lynx is a professional and he will not be dissuaded from doing his job.'

'How do you feel about him now?' Mildred enquired tentatively.

'I should hate him, but I just can't,' Melanie confessed. 'Elizabeth, Lon Mackeever and myself are meeting later this morning to discuss it. Hopefully, we will come up with a solution.'

'I pray that you will, Melanie.'

The sheriff had joined Melanie, Elizabeth, and Mackeever on their ride alongside a river to a rocky plateau a mile out of town. According to legend this was where the old trapper who had founded the town had named it after narrowly escaping the bite of a rattler. But legends and snake meant nothing to the serious-faced two men and two women as they dismounted that morning. The sun was a hot orange that pictured roaring flames on the water far below. An islet was like a verdant eel strung along the deep blue of the river.

Elizabeth Mackeever sighed. 'How can this lovely world be so horrible?'

'It's not the world, Elizabeth,' her husband said. 'It's the people who inhabit it.'

'So you are blaming Roscoe Lynx?' Melanie heard herself say in a challenging accusing way. Her feelings for Roscoe Lynx had even her loyalties confused.

'That's not so, Melanie,' Mackeever defended himself.

'Surely you are not saying it's our father's fault, Lon?' a horrified Elizabeth asked. 'It was Major DeWitt who got Jim Cutler's ranch.'

An unhappy Melanie reminded her sister, 'We have to face facts, Elizabeth. I have seen the deed. DeWitt couldn't have taken the ranch from Cutler without Father's legal expertise.'

Sheriff Winters spoke for the first time since they had left their horses to stroll to the edge of the plateau. 'We don't need to know who is at fault, but must find a way to avert a tragedy.'

'Avert a murder, Mike,' Elizabeth said. 'As sheriff you can prevent that happening.'

'There is nothing the sheriff can do. I have to take care of this,' Lon Mackeever said quietly. 'Me'n Roscoe Lynx have become buddies, but my duty is to my wife and her family.'

Both girls looked at Mackeever hopefully, but the sheriff's grim words brought them back down to earth. Winters said, 'You call Lynx, Lon, and you'll wind up as dead.'

'You know me, Mike,' Mackeever said with a feeble grin. 'Pretty fast on the draw.'

'There's fast, and there's Lynx, Lon. Neither you nor me are a match for him.'

Elizabeth suggested, 'What if my father offers Lynx money, more money than someone is paying him to do this terrible thing?'

The sheriff shook his head. 'Lynx isn't the kind of man who can be bought, Elizabeth.'

'That's ridiculous,' Elizabeth snapped derisively. 'He's been bought to come here and kill my father. I find that abhorrent.'

'This is the West, darling,' Mackeever said. 'Maybe in fifty years' time a man such as Lynx will be ostracized. But right now the way he is isn't a lot different to the rest of us.'

Though Melanie could see the logic of this, she wasn't prepared to say so. Learning that her father was as fallible as the next man had altered her perceptions. She would do everything in her power to prevent her father being harmed, but found it impossible to condemn Roscoe Lynx.

'We don't seem to have come up with an answer,' she said.

'I don't think that we will,' Mike Winters said sadly.

Mackeever puzzled all three of them with an enigmatic, 'We'll see.'

Hearing his name called from the street below, Roscoe Lynx walked to the window of his hotel room. Lon Mackeever was there, signalling for him to open the window. Lynx knew what Mackeever wanted, and a feeling of deep sorrow swept over him. He regretted having stayed so long in the town, getting to know Melanie, Mildred Carter, Lon Mackeever, and the sheriff. The barn raising at the Edwards' homestead came close to him abandoning his old way of life. He had really enjoyed that evening, had liked having friends and being part of a community.

Mackeever was calling his name again. Opening the window, Lynx waited.

'I guess you haven't changed your mind about

meeting Judge Larne later today, Lynx?'

'I'll be meeting him, Mackeever.'

'Then you'll meet me first,' Mackeever said. 'Ten minutes, Lynx, out here in the street.'

'There's no call for you to mix into this, Mackeever.'

'You've left me no choice, Roscoe: the judge is my wife's father.'

'Will anything I say change your mind?' Lynx enquired.

'No.'

'Then I'll be down in ten minutes.'

Lynx closed the window.

Rattlesnake Rock waited in a state of high tension. In the safety of the sheriff's office, with a clear view of the street, Melanie had an arm tightly round her sister. Mike Winters stood anxiously behind them. He had strongly advised Mackeever against the action he was taking.

'That man will kill Lon, won't he?' There was a tremor in Elizabeth's voice.

'It won't come to that,' Melanie said, desperately wanting to believe her own words. 'Roscoe and Lon have become friends. Neither of them will want to shoot the other.'

She looked to where Mackeever lounged casually against the hitching rail outside of the Blue Star. More than ten minutes had gone by and there was no sign of Roscoe Lynx. She was beginning to hope that Lynx had decided against a showdown, when the door of the hotel opened and he stepped out. Lynx

151

paused on the sidewalk, then stepped down into the dusty street. Lon Mackeever did the same, and the two men walked the centre of the street, slowly closing the gap between them.

'Lynx.'

Judge Larne had called the name. In the street some yards behind Roscoe, holding his jacket open, the judge had a peacemaker shoved under his belt.

'Lynx,' the judge called again. 'Turn and face me.'

Continuing his slow walk, Lynx made no sign of having heard, and the judge shouted again, 'Turn and face me, Lynx, or, God forgive me, I will shoot you in the back.'

Deeply moved by her father's courage, knowing that he was determined to save the life of Elizabeth's husband, Melanie heard Lynx call back to the judge. 'Go ahead, Judge. Shoot me in the back. That's the only way you'll stop me.'

Judge Larne pulled his gun from his belt and aimed it at Lynx's departing back. His gun hand was trembling and he used his other hand to steady it. Then he suddenly dropped the peacemaker, clapped both hands over his face, and dropped to his knees in the street

By that time, Lynx and Mackeever had stopped, facing each other. Lynx said, 'It's your move, Lon.'

'No,' Mackeever shook his head. 'You make your play'

Don't be a fool, *amigo*,' Lynx pleaded.

Still Mackeever refused to make a move, and Lynx's hand flashed down to the butt of his

152

holstered gun. Melanie, Elizabeth and the sheriff held their breath as Lynx's gun cleared leather and was levelled at Mackeever. Though the lawyer had drawn a shade slowly, he shot first. Lynx's gun fell from his hand as he spun round and crashed face down in the dust.

With the others running with her, Melanie got there as Mackeever helped Lynx to his feet. He had been hit in the left shoulder and was bleeding badly. Bending to pick up Lynx's gun, Mackeever said, 'Well I'll be damned,' and showed the gun to the sheriff and the women. There were no bullets in the chamber.

They all looked in awe at Lynx, who had offered himself as a sacrifice rather than kill Lon Mackeever. It was Mackeever who spoke first. 'Thank God that I didn't kill you, Roscoe.'

Standing with his right hand holding his damaged shoulder, dark-red blood leaking out between his fingers, Lynx gave a crooked grin. 'I'm faster than you, Lon.'

'You're the fastest gun I've ever seen, Roscoe, and the bravest man I've ever known.' Sheriff Winters complimented him. 'Come on, let's have Doc Baron take a look at that shoulder.'

'No, there's no need,' Lynx said, walking away from them down the street to where Judge Larne was getting shakily to his feet.

Patting the dust from his clothing, the judge looked round hurriedly for his gun as he saw Lynx advancing unsteadily on him. Panicking, Melanie was about to run to her father to protect him, but the sheriff held her arm, stopping her. 'The judge is in no danger, Melanie.'

Coming to a halt in front of a trembling Judge Larne, Lynx said, 'Rest easy, Judge. You can go home safely to your wife and family.'

'Why are you sparing me, Lynx?'

Taking a long time to reply, Lynx then spoke in a slow, puzzled way. 'I'm danged if I truly know, Judge, but if you're stuck for someone to thank in your prayers, give your daughter Melanie a mention.'

Major DeWitt came out on the street to stand by the judge as Lynx walked off, making his way towards the hotel.

'Lynx,' Judge Larne called after him. 'I'll make it up to Jim Cutler.'

'I'll tell him,' Lynx said without looking back.

'We both will, Lynx, me and Judge Larne,' DeWitt raised his voice to say.

'Like I said, I'll tell him,' Lynx replied.

'Rattlesnake Rock has taken everything from him,' Melanie said tearfully, as they watched Lynx go round to the back of the hotel. They realized that he had earlier hitched his horse there, ready to leave. As he rode into the street, Lynx reined up to lean over in the saddle and pluck a white rose from a bush that was growing wild against the hotel wall.

Then he rode steadily up the street, pulling up his horse to look down at the little group collected round the sheriff. It seemed that he was about to speak, but he remained silent. He looked at

Melanie for a full minute, then lightly kicked the flanks of his horse and started away. When he reached the spot here Rita Duprez had died, he got down from his horse and gently laid the white rose on the ground.

With difficulty, he got back into the saddle and rode away as Melanie knew that he would, without looking back.

Swaying in the saddle, weak from loss of blood, Roscoe Lynx stopped his horse in the shade offered by a clump of willow trees some two miles out of town. Easing one foot out of the stirrup he brought the leg over the horse and half-tumbled to the ground. Sitting in the dust, he weakly shuffled on his buttocks until his back rested against the trunk of a tree. Closing his eyes, he immediately fell into a sleep of exhaustion.

The sound of an approaching buckboard wakened him. He was reaching for his gun when his blurred vision made out a woman up high on the buckboard seat, reining up. Head swimming, he was aware of her dismounting and coming to kneel beside him. He caught the fragrance of her and heard her ask, as if from a far distance, if he had a knife. Using a little twist of his hip to indicate where his knife was in its scabbard of his belt, he felt her cutting his shirt away from his injured shoulder. There came the sound of her tearing material, and then his discomfort was eased as she deftly bound his shoulder.

She then held a canteen to his mouth and he

drank eagerly. Feeling better, he managed to focus on the figure in front of him. He tried to smile, and Mildred Carter smiled back at him.

'Hush,' she said. 'Rest awhile, and then I'll help you up on to the buckboard. I've already hitched your horse up behind.'

'Where are we going?'

'Wherever you say.'

Gaining strength, he reached for her hand and held it. 'Rattlesnake Rock was a turning point for me, Mildred, but life up ahead could be pretty rough.'

''It will be easier because we will face it together,' she said firmly.